If It's The Last Thing I Do

If It's The Last Thing I Do

The story of two friends who let a childhood
prank keep them apart for most of their lives.

Mark Francis

IF IT'S THE LAST THING I DO
THE STORY OF TWO FRIENDS WHO LET A CHILDHOOD
PRANK KEEP THEM APART FOR MOST OF THEIR LIVES.

iUniverse books may be ordered through booksellers or by contacting:

iUniverse
1663 Liberty Drive
Bloomington, IN 47403
www.iuniverse.com
1-800-Authors (1-800-288-4677)

*Because of the dynamic nature of the Internet, any web addresses or links contained in
this book may have changed since publication and may no longer be valid. The views
expressed in this work are solely those of the author and do not necessarily reflect the
views of the publisher, and the publisher hereby disclaims any responsibility for them.*

*Any people depicted in stock imagery provided by Thinkstock are models,
and such images are being used for illustrative purposes only.
Certain stock imagery © Thinkstock.*

ISBN: 978-1-4917-5272-2 (sc)
ISBN: 978-1-4917-5273-9 (e)

Library of Congress Control Number: 2014920027

Printed in the United States of America.

iUniverse rev. date: 11/17/2014

Chapter 1

As Max approached the exit where he had agreed to meet his childhood friend, he reflected back on the number of times he had passed this exit on his drive into the metro area, and all the chaos that entailed, and had not paid any attention to what was here. A small strip mall that he couldn't remember being built; offices for companies he had never heard of and the large fuel stop for cars, trucks and RV's. But mostly it was for trucks.

He thought about the time long ago when he moved to California and all there was here for buildings was a small gas station and a couple of mom and pop businesses. The realization that it had been forty years ago was something that he found hard to grasp. Where had the time gone? He remembered the construction, that had been such an inconvenience, to make the old two-lane highway into part of the greatest achievement of the modern world; the interstate freeway system. Copied from the German Autobahn system it allowed a driver to; except for fuel stops; drive from one coast of America to the other without having to stop for a stop sign or traffic signal. Shortly after he arrived in California he bought a small house (out in the sticks) as his fellow workers always said. After a couple years the two-lane road was upgraded to a four-lane; and sometime after that it was integrated into that marvel of modern engineering affectionately called the BIGROAD. The construction had been such an ongoing nightmare that it had become routine. Now twenty years after its completion the drive had become so routine that the world outside the barrier walls had ceased to exist for him. The countryside had progressed and changed but his life remained isolated from it. He worked for the same law firm he started with after graduating college, content with the security of a good income and bonuses. His home had grown along with his income and family but he had not moved from the original property he had bought when he and his wife had moved to California from Minnesota four decades ago.

Minnesota, just the thought of it made him shiver a little and check the thermometer on his dash to make sure it was still California comfortable outside.

His life growing up in Minnesota had been very Tom Sawyerish. During the summer it was bike riding every day, playing hide and seek at night, with no fear of who was seeking him. He trapped Pocket Gophers out of the hay field to earn a little spending money by turning them in for the bounty.

His life rolled on like a slow motion rollercoaster. Emotional highs, like getting the bike he wanted for his birthday; and soul crushing lows like when his dog and constant companion was ran over by a motorist who did not even slow down after hitting him. That incident could have been the seed planted in his mind that took root and became the driving force to find justice and try to right wrongs; and eventually go to law school and become a lawyer. It may have but at the time he was just pissed. The driver did not slow down or even try to swerve to avoid hitting the dog; and for a young boy that was wrong and he never forgot it.

He had been on his way to Willie's house to spend the day together as they always did when the chores were done. That day he did not go to Willies, and for several days after the incident he stayed home and did not want to see anyone. Eventually the pain grew less and He and Willie began their old routine of fishing and bike riding.

The day finally arrived when he was old enough to get his learners permit for a driver's license. It was just a formality for him because like all farm kids he had been driving machinery and pickup trucks since he was old enough to reach the peddles, and see over the hood. A driver's license was the beginning of a new phase of his life, but sadly it was the beginning of the end for one of the happiest times of his life.

Being a couple months older than Willie, Max had his license before Willie. He found an old car that he could afford and the two of them began venturing farther to find good fishing spots and also began spending more time in town hanging out. Willie was not always in favor of going into town wanting instead to spend more time in the country; fishing or just hiking in the woods. This eventually began to lead to disagreements and they began to see less of each other.

The two of them were still close but were now walking side by side on parallel paths instead of side by side on the same path. Soon the twists and turns of life would take them down very different paths.

One of these turns would eventually lead to the one incident that Max has regretted since it happened. The childish, spur of the moment prank that would haunt him his entire adult life. The twists, bends and turns in their lives caused their paths to cross many times. The turns of fate that lead them to this incident started when Willie got his license and did not have to depend on Max for rides. Willies father decided to retire from milking and sold all of the cattle. Without chores to do Willie was able to get a job. He got a job with a construction company in a neighboring town. For Willie it was great. Having no chores to do he could spend his days off from work fishing or hunting; depending on the season. To get to work he had bought an old pickup truck. It wasn't much but it was pure Willie. Max worked for a publishing company in a larger city farther away. He drove farther to work, had a newer car and made more money than Willie.

Max worked fewer hours than Willie but he drove farther and had to change into "fishing" clothes when he got home. This meant that Willie was usually already fishing by the time Max arrived. When Max arrived at the place they had agreed meet at there would be the usual greeting; Max would call Willie a slacker because he always got there first and Willie would call Max a workaholic for being so late. Then they would get into the business at hand.

Hunting was a more serious pastime for them. If they shot a squirrel, grouse or deer it was the end of the animals life and they shared the same feelings, waste not want not; they would process the animal carefully and divide the meat equally and both would take it home and put it in the freezer for a tasty meal in the future.

Fishing on the other hand was just fun. They both enjoyed the taste of a pan fried Trout or batter fried Bass fillets, but they were both very good at catching them so it didn't take them long to catch their limit and they fished so often that they could both fill a freezer in very little time. But they usually let them go to get a little bigger. They still used worms and other natural bait preferring to leave the fancy lures to the people who needed artificial help to catch a fish. They never entered any contests believing that to fish for money and glory cheapened the thrill of catching a "Big One".

Their competition was a simple shared rivalry without physical rewards. If one of them caught an exceptionally big fish and needed help landing it the other would put down their pole and help land it. There was no need to ask, it was the way it was. They would both admire the fish and check to see how deep it was hooked. If the hook could be removed without lasting harm to the fish they would throw it back with words like "I'm not keeping that little minnow" or "Run along home and get your big brother". Then they would go back to their poles and resume the serious business of catching fish.

They both agreed that the fish stayed fresher and got bigger in the water, something they didn't do in the freezer. Besides they could always catch a fresh fish if they wanted a meal.

Life was good for the two kids in rural Minnesota. A little money in their pocket, a little gas in their tank, and a lot of summer left before school started.

School was the one place they differed. Willie saw it as a necessary evil needed to get a piece of paper he could show a possible employer when he went looking for a job. No plans for college, he already knew who his employer was going to be it was just a matter of choosing which branch of the military he was going into.

Max had very different ideas. He saw school as a way to get a good job, avoid the military and live a comfortable life. Not the comfort of a soft pile of grass on a creek side, in the sun, but the comfort of a sturdy house to keep him warm when the sun wasn't shining. He always told Willie to learn a lot about construction so he could build him his house. Willie said Max would never make enough money to be able to afford his skill and expertise. Then they would bait their hooks and fish in silence; each lost in their own thoughts.

The summer before their senior year was uneventful almost to the point of routine boredom. Willie worked construction, Max published papers and they fished.

One of the clients of the publishing company was a law firm in the building next door. One of Max's jobs at the publishing company was to deliver the finished orders to the customers. This led him into contact with the people working in the business of law, and eventually into a friendship with a younger member of the firm. This friendship was the germinating force which brought to life a seed planted many years before. A seed that had been dormant for many years, buried under many layers of experiences; which now sprouted and grew into a desire to go into a career in the business of law. The one thing that nurtured the seed of thought was the life style the lawyers lived. A lifestyle Max could get used to very quickly. Justice was good but a fat pocketbook would be great. When he finally made the decision the switch careers he went to the personnel office of the law firm and filled out an application for a job, any job, just so he could get foot in the door of his now chosen profession.

Willie wasn't surprised when Max told him what he had decided to do. "You still won't be able to afford my skill and expertise to build your house", he said. Willie was a good worker, used to hard physical labor. He performed his duties quickly and efficiently never complaining and always smiling. His coworkers said he smiled like he was hiding a secret. He said the only secret he was hiding was where the best fishing was. Then he would smile and go back to work.

The days of their last "free" summer, as they called it, passed to quickly. They both realized when next summer came around their Tom Sawyer life style would be over and they would join the millions of workers competing for their slice of the American dream pie.

The company Willie worked for had gotten the contract to build an addition onto a local canning factory. It was a large job and gave the company work for the entire summer, and if completed on time, a very big bonus for the owners of the company; which they were going to divide up and share with the workers.

With the promise of a shared bonus and extra money for the early completion of the job, everyone on the crew worked harder and longer hours to get the job done as quickly as possible. There were concerns by some of the older workers, the ones with more experience, that they were going too fast, but the younger members of the crew just laughed and said that if they couldn't keep up just sit back out of the way and they would show them how to make extra money. As things turned out the concerns of the more experienced workers were well founded and hindsight being what it is the words "I guess we should have listened", were heard quite a lot.

The day for Willie started out like every other day at work. He got up early; early enough to start the coffee for his parents who after years of getting up long before sunrise to start chores enjoyed sleeping in a little later.

He made himself breakfast, packed a lunch and checked the worms he had dug the night before. The weather forecast had called for rain and Willie was holding them to it. He hadn't had a day off for fishing for weeks and he was looking forward to getting rained out of work today. The day at work started out like most days, but it would end very different.

He had been working a lot of overtime on the job because the company owners wanted to finish before the fall rains started and slowed their progress down. Getting home late, Working Saturdays and family obligations had meant he hadn't been able to go fishing much. He told Max he thought he was going through withdrawal.

Today the weather was predicted to change and a large thunderstorm was supposed to roll through in the afternoon. That meant he might get done work early and even though he couldn't work in the rain, he could always fish in the rain. At work rain made things miserable. While fishing he called it liquid sunshine.

As the day wore on the sun and heat were oppressive; the humidity was so high that Willie joked with his fellow a worker that the fish might be able to swim in the air and come to him if he couldn't get to them. The guy looked at him and said he really needed to seek professional help for his addiction. Willie said if it rained he was going to therapy that night at his favorite fishing spot. By noon a slight breeze had began to blow and Willie knew form watching the weather on the farm that he was going fishing that afternoon.

The breeze was a welcome relief and cooled things down a little. The men worked a little faster, and work progressed a little faster. As things turned out maybe a little too fast. They were laying blocks on one of the longer walls of the addition and the foreman put all the block layers on the one wall. The courses of blocks went up fast and the scaffolding crew was kept busy raising the scaffolding to the next level. Willies job as mud tender was to mix the cement used to set the blocks in place. The heat and now the breeze were constantly drying the mud out and Willie worked constantly to supply the block layers he was assigned to with fresh mortar so they could keep laying blocks. The higher the scaffolding went the more difficult his job became. He thought it was ironic that the word slacker came from his job. When the cement was mixed it was supposed to be left to sit for a couple minutes, a processes known as letting the mud go slack. If they weren't real busy and the mud tenders didn't have to carry the mud very far they would just wait for the couple minutes and so the term slacker was applied to any worker that was seen standing around not appearing to be doing anything. Willie didn't have to worry about being called that today. By the time he had climbed the scaffolding and returned to the mixer the mud had sat long enough and he would empty the mixer into a pail, mix another batch and start climbing back up. On one of his trips he stopped on the top of the scaffolding to catch his breath and enjoy the breeze which didn't reach him on the ground. He noticed clouds on the western horizon and he knew salvation in the form of a couple hours of fishing was a sure thing. He also noticed a small whirlwind, called a dust devil coming across a field, kicked up by the increasing breeze, which was beginning to be not a breeze but a light wind.

He heard a couple of the older more experienced block layers talking when he delivered mortar to them about how dangerous it was to put a wall up this fast because the mortar in the joints didn't get a chance to cure before more weight was added on top of it. They called it a green wall and said it was an accident waiting to happen.

Max was a happy boy. When he arrived at work there was a letter on his desk. He opened it and read the words he had been waiting for. He had been accepted for a job at the law firm next door. He was smiling when he looked up and noticed his boss standing beside him. "I hate to lose you; you're a good worker, but I knew you were not going to stay here for long. Good luck on your new career", and with that Max was on his way to becoming an attorney. He couldn't wait to tell Willie. His job didn't depend on the weather and there was little opportunity for working overtime. Getting off work early had given him opportunity to go fishing more often than Willie, but he has found excuses to do other things. What's the fun in catching a big fish if there's no one to help land it and to brag to about catching it. He had heard the weather forecast and was excited about the possibility of Willie getting off early and the two of them going fishing and maybe stopping for a burger at the drive-in.

Willie opened his eyes. The room above him was white and the lights glaringly bright. He tried to move his head but it felt like it was trapped in a vice. Just as he was about to scream in pain a face loomed over his. The tear streaked face of his mother. He felt her hand holding his and heard her reassuring voice telling him that everything was alright. That was enough to quiet his panic, but it did nothing to ease the confusion he was feeling. The room suddenly got very busy. As the doctors and nurses suddenly began checking him over from top to bottom. Now that he was awake he could answer their questions about how he was feeling. And ask questions they did; so many questions and so quickly he didn't know which one to answer first. After the initial rush they began to slow down and became a little less urgent in their questioning. They asked how he felt, if he could move his toes, if he had pain anywhere, if he knew what day it was, did he know his name, did he know what happened, did he know where he was, could he feel this poke. The questions kept coming and he moved his eyes from one face to the next trying to make sense out of, what to him was a senseless situation. The panic began to return and then his mothers face reappeared and he calmed down. "Willie, you've been hurt in an accident on the job. You're in the hospital. You have fractured bones in your neck." The tears fell down like raindrops landing on the sheet covering his chest. Willie's mind was trying to sort out all of the things he had just heard and it became so overwhelming his mind recoiled from the overload and he started drifting off to sleep. After the quick examination and with the answers to their question confirming no additional injuries the doctors had decided that rest was the best medicine right now and had given him a sedative to make him sleep. His only injury was a big one; a fractured neck.

Willie became aware of voices and pain. He didn't open his eyes but instead he listened. He laid with his eyes closed and his mind in fast forward trying to make sense out of what his mother had said. He thought back to what he remembered last. Putting the mortar on the mud board and taking a short break to enjoy the breeze that he was sure was bringing him a chance to go fishing. He remembered looking at the clouds gathering on the horizon and their promise of getting off work early. He thought about the dust devil and thinking that because it was spinning counter clockwise it was a sure sign of rain. Clockwise rotation meant dry weather; at least that is what he had told himself still hoping for an early day and some fishing.

Then he opened his eyes and said "Oh, no". His mother thinking something was wrong with him called for the nurse, but a familiar voice said "don't worry; I put them in the garden".

Leave it to Max to read his thoughts. Max had heard about the accident and went to the construction site to see if Willie was alright and if there was anything he could do to help. He had to park a ways from the site because it was total chaos with emergency vehicles, paramedics, construction workers and most of the townspeople all moving in different directions; and Max didn't want to get in the way. As he stood there looking at the scene in front of him he had a hard time figuring out what he was looking at and what had happened. The metal scaffolding was twisted and bent, imbedded in piles of cement blocks, with more blocks scattered everywhere, people were running, limping, walking, crying and just standing and looking with shocked expressions. Police and rescue vehicles with sirens and lights going were coming in and leaving out on every street. He saw rescue vehicles from two neighboring towns, plus all the fire and rescue vehicles from his hometown, all trying to clear the scene. He realized that whatever had happened it was big and had affected a lot of people. All he had been told was that a wall had fallen and Willie might have been injured.

At a loss as to what he should do Max wandered around in the background away from the chaos around the collapsed wall. He walked towards the parking lot and remembered their plans to go fishing after work.

He knew Willie would have his worms dug to save time, and get to the fishing spot faster.

He went to Willie's pickup and tried the door; it was locked. He reached into his pocket and pulled out his keys and separated out the one that fit Willie's truck. The two of them had given each other a key to their vehicle as soon as they had bought them. He opened Willie's door and looked around inside until he spotted the worm cooler on the passenger floor covered with a jacket. He picked it up and started towards his own vehicle.

It is said that all fishermen are superstitious and Willie and Max were no exception. Some have to wear a certain hat or a "lucky" shirt. Others only fish on certain days; some have a special lure or pole that they have to use. Willie never admitted to any superstitions claiming it was patience and practice that enabled him to catch fish, but he did have one ritual that he always practiced.

The worms he used came from around the cattle yard on his dad's farm. The ground was rich and loose from years of composting manure. The worms were plentiful and big, "just what the fish want", he would tell Max. The first part of the ritual was never taking a small worm. "Big worms big fish". The second part was after fishing to always return the worms to his mother's garden.

Since his parents had retired from farming and sold the cattle his ritual had changed a little. First, it was no longer his mother's garden. It was now the combined effort of both his mom and dad. Without the cattle and crops to keep him busy Willies dad had started helping with the growing of vegetables. He moved the garden into the old cattle lot and instead of weeds it now grew row after row of vegetables. It was planted so full Willie was forced to confine his worm gathering to the outer edges of the lot. Even on the edges he had to be careful not to disturb a berry bush or newly planted fruit tree.

Although his father had turned the cattle lot into the garden, Willie still returned the worms to the spot his mother maintained. Only now it grew mostly flowers and flowering shrubs.

It was to this spot that Max carried the cooler of worms he had taken from Willies truck. There was no one home as they were at the hospital with Willie. So Max went around to the back of the house; a walk he had made with Willie many times. He opened the door to a small garden shed reached to the left and removed a short handled fork from its hook. He walked to the flower garden and found a spot that didn't have plants growing in it and dug a small hole. He dumped the worms in it and crumbled the dirt back over them. He then stood up and looked around at the well tended home site and thought about all the times he and Willie had performed this very act together. He walked to the water hydrant and washed off the fork and returned it to its hook in the shed closed the door and walked to the garage to put the cooler in its spot on the shelf then he turned towards his car. He walked slowly dreading where he was going and worried about what he might find when he got there.

Before he went to the hospital there was one more stop Max had to make. He drove to the spot they had planned to fish at and took a cooler from the back seat of his car.

Although Max lived on the farm next to Willie he had a different childhood. His father was a crop farmer and his mother worked in town so there was no garden plot on the place to put his worms in. Max had developed his own ritual for disposing of his unused worms. He had a favorite spot where he dug his worms but instead of returning the ones left after fishing he would toss them into the stream where they had been fishing. He told Willie he was personally responsible for the large size of the fish they caught. As he stood there watching the fish grab the worms as they floated to the bottom he wondered if he and Willie would ever fish together again. He didn't know how bad Willie was injured but he had been told it was a neck injury. Tossing the last of the worms into the water he turned and walked slowly back to his car. He had stalled his trip to the hospital knowing that there would be a lot of confusion and he didn't want to get in the way. He also wanted to give the doctors time to find out the extent of Willies' injuries so he didn't have to sit in that place not knowing if he would ever walk again.

Willies' mother looked at Max and said, "What on earth are you talking about?"

A tired voice from the bed said "The worms, right?" and Max nodded. "We were going fishing after work if Willie got rained out. I knew that wasn't going to happen now so I took the worms out of Willies' pickup and put them in your garden." Max explained, as he stood looking at Willie.

Tears began flowing down the cheeks of Willies' mother. Tears of relief, tears of joy, tears of worry and just tears of a mother seeing her son injured and not knowing what to do to make him better. All those emotions flowing from her eyes down her cheeks and on to the handkerchief Max handed her to catch them. Max stepped forward and gave her a hug just because he knew Willie wanted to but couldn't.

While daubing at her eyes and with a voice that caught and faltered Willies' mother managed to say "You two don't need a medical doctor you need a shrink." But she was relieved beyond measure to know that the fall and subsequent injuries hadn't hurt Willies mind. The body can heal she told herself.

His body did heal. A couple days in the hospital and Willie was released, or as one nurse put it "he was uncaged." Willie did not take very good to his role as patient. Walking the halls of the hospital when he was told to stay in bed. Watching television when he was told it was time for sleep. His was a happy day when they told him he could go home. He had heard the nurses comment about him being uncaged and he asked them to uncage his head, but they told him the halo would have to stay on until the doctor said it could come off. Willie told her he had tools at home and he could get it off by himself. She said in alarm that he had better not try or he would end up with a worse condition than he had now. He winked and said "just kidding." The nurse blushed and turned away, a little ashamed that she had let her personal feelings toward Willie show. Behind all of her complaining and scolding she liked Willie. She liked him more than just as a patient and didn't want him to see it

By he time school started in the fall Willie had healed and the halo had been removed. He had managed to get Max to take him fishing a couple times and the doctors had finally decided that the thing was probably going to cause more harm than good in Willies' case. After reviewing the x-rays he said the words Willie had been waiting impatiently to here, "We're taking the cage off."

While waiting in the office for the doctor to come in and remove the halo Willie started thinking back to the day of the accident. He had found out from talking to the other workers who were on the wall at the time of the collapse what had happened. While most of the block layers and tenders were on the top layer of the scaffolding; Willie happened to be on the ground but still under the structure. There were a few workers not yet punched in and a few spectators standing around but they were out of reach of the wall when it fell. The dust devil Willie had noticed in the field had kept growing as it came towards the wall until it became; what one worker described it as; a white tornado. It had hit the wall with enough force and at the right place to actually cause it to fall over. Taking the scaffolding and workers with it. The workers on the top got a very frightening ride but were thrown clear of the danger. The few workers like Willie who were under or in the scaffolding were the ones that received the worst injuries. When the collapse started Willie was still lost in thoughts of an early day off and going fishing, he was late noticing what was happening and unlike most of the people who ran he was caught by falling blocks and planks from the four layers of scaffolding. Although his injuries were serious they could have been a lot worse. The frame of the scaffolding actually shielded him from most of the falling objects and protected him from being buried under a pile of forty pound blocks. A fractured neck was serious but he couldn't help thinking what might have happened, and he shivered every time he thought about having been paralyzed.

"The old guys were right", he thought. The wall went up too fast and a strong wind was able to knock it over.

Two things came out of the accident for Willie; one was a fractured neck and the other was the fact that he couldn't smell. He hadn't said anything at first, thinking the problem would go away and his sense of smell would return. After a few weeks he mentioned it to his mom; she said he should have said something right away because the doctors might be able to do something about it. On his next visit to the hospital he was mobbed by a team of nerve specialists. After they studied charts and asked him a lot of questions they came to the conclusion, based on their learned and professional opinion, that there had been some kind of nerve damage and he had lost the connection between his olfactory sensory organ and the section of the brain that analyzes the information. They had never had a case like this before and didn't know if it would be permanent or if it would mend itself. "Brilliant", Willie thought, "they don't know if it will come back or if any other nerves will show up as damaged, but after four hours of examination they confirmed that he couldn't smell."

Another result of the wall incident affected both Max and Willie, and their friendship. The law firm Max worked for was hired by the factory to defend it against lawsuits as a result of the accident. The factory owners put the responsibility totally on the construction company for not following safety standards. The fact that Willie worked for the construction company and Max worked for the law firm representing the factory created a conflict of interest and the two were told they could not have contact with each other until the case was settled. The two boys took it as a joke but Max's boss showed them how serious the matter was when he threatened to fire Max after finding out they had been fishing together.

By the time the lawsuits were all settled the summer was over and school was started. The two friends who were always together were now moving in different social circles. Willie fished alone most of the time and Max, who joined the football team, spent more time with that crowd.

The crowd Max hung around with were mostly the more popular kids in school from the more prominent families. They accepted Max because of his job and career choice, but they looked down on Willie as just another manual laborer. This caused a bigger divide in their friendship and eventually led Max to do the one stupid stunt that he would regret the rest of his life; and would cause the split in their relationship that would last the rest of their lives. The stunt was a dare from the guys he played ball with and Max went along with it trying to impress them and show he was part of the "team".

With his one good friend now occupied with a different circle of friends Willie had changed a little also. After fishing he went to the drive-in more often just to hang-out. He was parked at the drive-in on a Friday night when a car pulled into the parking spot next to him. He glanced at the driver and recognized her as a girl from a neighboring town. He looked at the other passengers and his eyes locked on a pair of eyes in the back seat that were looking at him. It was the "nurse" who had joked that he was being uncaged when he was released from the hospital. She quickly turned away and Willie saw the same crimson color flush her cheeks.

That casual glance played over and over in his head over the next few days until he finally asked around to find out what her name was.

He found out her name was Jean and that she wasn't a nurse, but had been working in the hospital as an aid. She was actually his age and a senior from a town a couple miles away. After getting up the nerve to approach her and talk to her they became friends and Willie eventually asked her if she would go with him to his senior prom. She agreed but only if he would accompany her to her prom. He agreed and the stage was set for what Max would refer to as his "stupid move" for the rest of his life.

Willie put up with a lot of ridiculing because of the fact he couldn't smell. It was the source of great entertainment for some of the other kids who would put something rotten in a bag and have him smell it, and then have a big laugh when he didn't react. They really aren't too bright, he would think after each incident. They have to put up with the smell just to make fun of me for not being able to.

The day of the prom Willie spent hours cleaning and waxing his pickup. His parents thought it would be better if he used their car but he insisted that he was going to use his own vehicle and that there was nothing wrong with a pickup truck for a prom vehicle.

On the way to pickup his date Willie stopped at the local florist to get a corsage for Jean. He had argued with his mom that he just wanted to pick a couple flowers out of her garden to use but she had insisted that a girl wants a nice corsage to keep as a reminder of her senior prom.

While Willie was in the store Max pulled up and parked behind his truck.

Max swung his car off the freeway down the ramp and turned onto the access road to the truck stop. "Maybe I should just drive by", he thought. "I haven't seen this guy in over forty years. The last time I talked to him was at senior prom when he yelled "I'll get even with you if it's the last thing I do". Then Max started thinking about the "stupidest thing" he had ever done. He turned into the truck stop and pulled into the parking spot Willie had told him to park in; turned off the ignition and sat there with his hands resting on the steering wheel as if he were bracing himself for some kind of an impact.

Park in the last space, on the west end, of the first row, by the restaurant. I will be parked in the first spot on the east end of the front row of trucks. It had sounded simple enough when Willie told him, but now that he was actually in the parking lot Max wondered how Willie could have known that the parking spaces he indicated would be empty when they both got there. The parking lot for the automobiles and campers covered four or five acres alone and when he looked out over the sea of trucks he was awe struck by the vastness of the place. Trucks of all make, model, and color; hooked to trailers of different size and designed for different functions. He had heard that the American distribution system was the greatest achievement of the modern world; and looking at just this one small part of that system he got some idea of what it took to keep the system functioning.

The parking lot for automobiles was built on a hill that had been leveled on top and paved over, but was still about fifty feet above the lot where the trucks parked. From his car Max could look out over the rows of trucks but could not see the ones directly below him. "I sure wish I would have asked Willie more details about his truck." Max began to worry that if Willie was not parked in the spot he had said he was going to be that he would never find him in that jungle of steel and rubber that continually changed as trucks left and new ones arrived. Max was beginning to feel a little intimidated by this new world he found himself in. A world he had only experienced as he drove down the freeway and became irritated because one of these trucks was in front of him and he couldn't see around it.

It was five o'clock in the morning and Max had not had any coffee or breakfast yet. His daily routine had been totally disrupted. He felt very uncomfortable wearing work boots and blue jeans but Willie had told him not to show up in a suit and tie. Max hadn't worn blue jeans for quite a while. His lifestyle had advanced to khakis and polo shirts as leisure wear. He felt awkward but noticed all the people walking past; and even at this early hour there were quite a few people walking around; were wearing "T" shirts, blue jeans and either tennis shoes or work boots. After watching the people around him for awhile he only felt uncomfortable because his clothes were new. He had went out and bought three pairs of blue jeans, three "T" shirts and a pair of workboats because he actually did not own any.

After twenty minutes of sitting in his car and people watching he finally decided it was time to try to find this kid that he hadn't seen in over forty years. He thought about calling his wife Sue, just to get a little reassurance but decided not to wake her. She had been very enthusiastic about him going on this insane adventure and was the deciding factor that put him in this parking lot.

Looking out the passenger window over the rows of trucks Max wondered how it would be possible for Willie to park in the one specific parking space he had told Max he would be. Again he wished he would have paid more attention to Willie when he had described his truck; but at the time he hadn't thought he would actually go along with this idea. Now that he was here he tried hard to remember all that Willie had said.

"Get out of your car; follow the sidewalk down the steps. I'll be the first truck in the first row to your left front." That is what he had said. Max tried to remember what he had said the name on the truck would be. He thought it was Round something or other but couldn't remember positively.

After a few more moments of thought and confidence building Max opened his car door into a world that was totally alien to him. Even at this early hour it was a world of noise and activity. He stepped out, opened the trunk and swung the strap of his larger bag over his shoulder and grabbed the handles of his smaller bag, closed the trunk and turned to face the jungle of trucks. Ok he thought just look for a tall skinny kid with a big smile; what can be so hard about that? He walked the edge of the hill where the steps began and realized there were only two or three trucks in each row that he had not been able to see from his car. He looked down and just as he had feared the first truck in the first row to his left front was not Willie. The driver had the hood open and was standing on the frame by the engine washing the windshield. The truck was not shinny like most of the others and from where he was standing it certainly wasn't Willie cleaning that glass. The guy had old coveralls on and the hair showing from under the ball cap he was wearing was grey-white not brown like Willie's

He looked at the trailer and caught a small patch of words in the lower front corner. "Round-a-bout trucking" that's what Willie had said his trucking company was called. Max thought maybe he had more than one truck and this was another driver sent to meet him because Willie was unable to be there at the time he had told Max to be there.

Then Max looked back at the driver who was climbing down from the frame where he had been washing the windows. This couldn't be Willie Max thought. Willie would have jumped down and this guy was moving very slow, looking for handholds and footholds.

Max looked at the truck, it wasn't real old but it hadn't been washed or polished for quite a while. Max didn't know the different kinds of trucks and from this distance he couldn't read the name on the side, but as he was looking at it he thought back to Minnesota and the days of fishing and fun. The pickup Willie drove back then was old when he bought it. He had bought it from a neighbor who had parked it in back of his barn when he bought a new one. It was customary for farmers to keep their old equipment and not trade it in when they replaced it. A lot of farms had a lot "out back" where they parked the used equipment, and Willie had spotted it and fell in love with it immediately.

Willie had bought the pickup in late summer and spent that fall and most of the winter working on it in the corner of his dads' machine shed. Max had jokingly asked if he had bought it to drive or just to have something to work on. Willie said he was too impatient and that he would drive plenty when it was finished. And drive it he did. The day he showed up in town the following spring he got every ones attention.

Not many of the kids customized their vehicles in those days. They usually bought one that was ready to drive, not one out of a scrape pile. While most kids were satisfied with a little shag carpet on the dash or some dice hanging from the rear view mirror, Willie was the exception; he had completely restored the body of the old International pickup. Every dent, scratch and ding had been removed and any rusted area had been cut out and new metal had been welded in... The motor and entire drive train had been removed disassembled, new parts put in and then the whole assembly had been painted with a rustproof paint. He had bought new tires with a very wide white side wall stripe, reupholstered the seat, put in new floor coverings, replaced the inside door panels because he couldn't get the original ones clean enough to suit him. Then he had painted the entire pickup. The paint job was what got every ones attention.

Willie had found some used cans of paint in his dads shed that were about half full each. There wasn't enough of either to paint the pickup so Willie decided to mix the two colors together. He thought he had heard someplace that if yellow and green were mixed together the result would be blue. He was wrong; blue is a primary color and cannot be made from other colors being mixed. The result of mixing yellow and green is lime green, but in Willies case it was hard to tell if it was yellow green or green yellow. Willie had been planning on painting the truck blue but decided that instead of wasting the paint he had created he would use it on his truck. The one he had just spent over half a year reconditioning. Although everyone who saw the truck called it lime green they were never quite sure if that was a true description of the color. The one thing they all agreed on was that it really shined. After two coats of paint and a couple coats of clear finish Willie had spent several hours waxing his pickup. He waxed and polished the entire truck, including the inside of the cargo box.

Willie had said that there wasn't a bolt, screw or pin in the entire truck that he hadn't removed inspected replaced if it was worn or rusted, but that fact was forgotten when people saw the color it was painted, but when Max thought back he remembered one thing about the pickup; it always shined.

That was the one thing that convinced him the person climbing down from the frame of the truck he was looking at was not Willie; the truck did not shine.

When the driver finally reached the ground and turned towards him Max was surprised to see an older Willie looking at him. He just stared for a moment a then fast forwarded to the present.

The world Max lived in was a world of illusion and deception. If he was unsure of a case he was working on he had to put on the illusion of confidence to deceive the opposing attorney and the jury. Part of the deception was appearance. He dyed his hair to hide the grey. Worked out to keep fit and avoid the mid-life mid-section bulge that could be seen as a sign of weakness. With all of this deception in his professional life he had forgotten that his personal life clock had continued and that he was over sixty years old. With all the attention to maintaining a youthful appearance he looked youthful, but mature. Like Willies old pickup truck he really shined on the outside.

Looking down the hill at Willie he suddenly realized how many years had passed since he had left Minnesota to go where the money was, and where things were really happening. That was what he had told his parents when they had asked him why he wanted to move to California.

Willie smiled that big farm boy smile and waved; Max smiled and waved back and the years that had separated them melted away. The two farm boys were going on another fishing trip together. Instead of worms for bait they were going to use memories to catch something more elusive than a trout or bass. They were going fishing for an old friendship which had been swimming around just under the surface of their consciousness for over forty years.

The doorbell rang a Sue stopped what she was doing to answer it. Her first reaction was to check her appearance in the long hallway mirror. After years as the wife of a prominent attorney she was always aware of what effect her appearance had on her husbands' social standing. Like Max she had worked hard and spent much time and money to stay younger looking. Not to fight off the younger generation who were trying to take her job as max was; but to fight off an age old enemy; old age. She was pleased with what she saw in the mirror. With the help of cosmetics, surgery and high end department stores she still looked very young and attractive. High maintenance but highly worth it she thought. As she walked to answer the doorbell she had no idea how much her cultured life was about to change. Reaching down she opened the door.

It took a moment for her to recognize the person standing on her front steps, but in one sweeping glance her vision caught the person on the steps and then was directed to something on the street. At first it was just a color then a shape and then everything began to blur as the tears invaded her eyes.

In a quiet voice she said "Jean, you made it," and then she stepped forward to hug her oldest and dearest friend. For a long moment they hugged then stepped back from each other and clasped hands and looked at each others' faces; then all sense of social dignity vanished and they began squealing and bouncing up and down like two school girls at a high school dance.

When the excitement of seeing each other lowered to a manageable level and the bouncing and squealing stopped Sue invited her long time friend into her home for the first time. Before she followed she glanced one more time at the vehicle parked in the street in front of her house. It was an old International pickup truck painted a strange yellow green or green yellow, she never could decide which. "I can't believe you drove that old thing all the way from Minnesota. Actually, I can't believe that truck is still running." They were sitting in Sues' living room and she could see Willies' truck through the front window. "That truck is probably in better condition than half the vehicles on the road today," as she talked Jean turned to look at the old truck. When she turned back Sue caught a look in her eyes; just a fleeting look of something lost. "Including the first time he disassembled that truck Willie has taken it apart two more times. Wait until you see what he has done to the interior." As Jean spoke Sue again caught a fleeting glimpse of loss on her face.

Hours later the two of them were still sitting in the spacious living room of Sues' house. They had shared laughs, lunch and a lifetime of memories and were now quietly enjoying each others' company. Their conversations were interspersed with spaces of quiet contemplation as they would slip back to the memories of days of innocence when life was still an adventure and they were still in school.

Jean was thinking about the time in her junior year in high school when she had gotten a job in the hospital in a neighboring town. The town where Willie, Max and Sue lived, and where her life would take a turn into the future that would eventually bring her to California and the living room of her long time friend.

Sue and Jean had met at the local drive-in and became friends immediately. Sues' father owned the construction company where Willie worked and Sue spent her summers working in the office; helping her mother with the paperwork and running an occasional errand to the different job sites to deliver something to her father. On a few of these errands she had noticed a new kid working as a block tender for the men laying the blocks on the addition to a local canning company. She found out his name was Willie and that he was a fish-a-holic with not much interest in dating or socializing. Too bad, she thought he's kind of easy on the eyes.

When they had a day off together; which for Sue meant Sunday or a holiday, and for Jean; who worked a rotating shift, it was different days every week; they would spend them either at the drive-in or at the local swimming hole in a stream not far from town. The town had a municipal swimming pool but for the older kids the gathering spot was the "swimming hole". On weekends some of them would bring beer and after dark there would be a bonfire. There was always the possibility of the police showing up but that was all part of the excitement.

Sometimes an old International pickup would stop and two boys would get out and join the group. They were more interested in talking about fishing and never stayed very long. Sue recognized Willie from the job site and would blush a little if he happened to walk by and said hi. They never stayed very long when they did stop saying they were wasting good fishing time. Willie or his friend Max would say "let's go," they would climb into the pickup and be gone in a flash of green-yellow or yellow-green.

When the wall fell at the construction site and Willie was taken to the hospital part of Jeans' embarrassment was that she secretly had a crush on him. Although Sue had "Dibbs" on him because she was the first one to "discover" him she knew the way Jean looked at him she didn't stand a chance. Besides she said the other one was cuter anyway. Jean had talked to Sue about him and knew he worked for her dad and, knew his name and where he lived and anything else she could find out about him; almost to the point of stalking. She was working in the hospital the day of the accident and when he was brought to the emergency room on the gurney her heart skipped a beat when she saw him laying there bleeding from some minor cuts and his head immobilized. She wanted to go to him and hold his hand and let him know how she felt but his mother was already there and Jean knew better than to come between a mother and her injured child. She had thought about that incident many times over the years when Willie was gone over the road in his truck. She knew that was the moment that she had fallen in love with the gangly farm boy named Willie who's only passion at the time was fishing. Jean also knew she had a big job ahead of her trying to change his passion. Sue and Jean had talked about it and they reached the conclusion that it was a girls' job to domesticate the boys without letting them know they were being manipulated. Sue had already set her sights on Max and because of the accident she would get her chance to meet him and start the change happening.

After Max had transferred the worms from Willies' pickup to his car he had taken a few moments to wander around the construction site not knowing exactly what to do. From the background he watched the commotion as the last of the workers were being treated and the more seriously injured were loaded into ambulances and taken to the hospital. He watched a number of people go in and come out of a small trailer that was used as an onsite office by the construction company, and decided to go there to see if he could get any more information about Willies' condition. The trailer was empty when he opened the door except for a young girl sitting at a desk and talking on the phone. She hung up the phone when he opened the door and invited him to come in. Although she already knew who he was and why he was there she asked him anyway. She didn't want him to know that she had stayed behind because she knew Max would show up asking about Willie. She told him all she knew and that was that Willie had an injury to his neck and that it might be serious. Max thanked her and left. On the way to Willies' house to get rid of the worms Max kept thinking about the girl in the office trailer. He'd noticed her at school and around town but had never had time for dating or socializing but now with the possibility of Willie being seriously injured he felt lost and thought maybe after things settled down he might talk to her again; she had seemed very friendly and easy to talk to. Sues job was going to be a lot easier than Jeans.

As the days turned to months after the accident Sue and Max were seeing each other more often. With the lawsuit and it's restraint barring the boys from talking with each other the change had began that would send Sue to California and make Jean a truck drivers wife. The girls still met and talked whenever they could but with the start of school Jean spent more time in her hometown and less time working.

The boys were seeing less of each other and Willie began making the trip to see Jean in her hometown more and more often. It was only natural that Willie would ask her to prom and that she would gladly accept. She was very excited about the event and had absolutely no idea about the coming events at the flower shop or the events that were to follow. Events that would lead to this meeting in Sues house forty years later.

But that was a long time ago and this is now so she brought herself back to the present reality and the adventure her and Sue were about to embark on.

After a light lunch and hours of talk Sue took Jean on a tour of her spacious house. It was a combination tour and security check. As they looked in each room Sue would check to make sure that the windows were closed and locked all lights off and all appliances unplugged. She took a few minutes at the phone to transfer the home number to her cell phone and unplug the television. She had already backed up and shut down the computer, checked the basement and garage, so with a final look around she looked at Jean and said "lets' go for a ride".

Jean was a little concerned about Max noticing that the phone had been switched to Sues' cell phone; but Sue assured her it would be alright; she said that Max might be a high class lawyer but when it came to the new electronic gadgets he was quite intellectually challenged. He was not supposed to know that Jean had driven out to pick Sue up and that the two of them were driving back to Minnesota. Sue had convinced him that it would be a great opportunity for the two boys to reconnect after all these years, and after the trip and Max flew home then the four of them could plan a time when they could all get together.

If Max suspected anything he never let on. This was just going to be a two day road trip and then a night at a class reunion; this would be the first class reunion that he had attended since graduation. After the reunion he would fly home. He tried to get Sue to drive to Minnesota with him and then they could get together with Jean and Willie but Sue had convinced him that she had social engagements that she could not break and that it would be good for the two of them to patch things up by themselves.

With a final look around the house they each picked up a couple bags and stepped out onto the front steps and Sue turned and locked the door. Max and Sue lived in a gated community and there was very little concern about leaving the house unattended for a week. Although they weren't real close with their neighbors, as nobody in their community was real close, they all waved and watched out for each other. Everyone realized what happened to one could happen to any of them.

Sue had already talked to the security people and they would routinely check the property and the house. Jean wondered who checked on the security people, but that was just Jean who had lived with Willie for too many years.

As they walked to the pickup Sue had no worries about leaving her house unattended but she did have a few reservations about what she was about to do. She looked at the old International pickup truck and thought about how far it was to Minnesota and wondered if it was safe to get into a vehicle that old. Jean got an inkling of what she was thinking and told her all of the things Willie had done to the truck. She told her he had replaced the entire dash and all the instruments with a dash from a late model truck. She said he had even installed an entire air conditioning system using parts from several different models. He had also constructed a cargo carrier in the cargo box that she thought he should patent so he could get some money and retire. He had told her he didn't want the trouble of dealing with people who would just use the money they already had to rip him off by stealing his idea before it was legally patented because they had the funds to hire lawyers that he couldn't afford to fight against; And after a long and costly battle he would be left with nothing because they would probably take the cargo carrier out of his pickup saying he didn't own it. After she had went on about the lawyers and how they would rip Willie off she suddenly remembered who she was talking to and quietly said "sorry". Sue laughed and said "He's probably right, they probably would; but don't worry about saying it to me girl, I'm not the lawyer, I just spend the lawyers money." The two of them looked at each other and laughed like they used to laugh when they talked about the two boys who only understood fishing.

The first stop at the pickup was the tailgate to put the bags into Willies storage box. Jean pulled up on the handle to open the tail gate like she would on a regular pickup tailgate latch. That is where regular ended. Instead of folding down the tailgate swung open to the right side. It was thicker than a regular tailgate and on the inner surface there was a series of small compartments each with a latch and hinges recessed into the metal this gave the surface a smooth look and allowed it to fit closely to the structure built into the cargo bed. About five inches in from both sides of the end gate there were circular depressions in the metal. When the tail gate was closed these housed two metal rings that were attached to rails that slid under the structure filling the cargo box. Jean lifted the two rings and pulled out rails that slid out about three feet then hinged downward to rest on the ground at the bend in the legs there was a locking lever that Jean snapped into place so the legs were stable. On the front of the cargo box there were two handles recessed into the face, Jean lifted these handles and pulled the "drawer" out a short distance. As the drawer moved out two legs began to lower themselves to the ground. On the end of the legs there were small wheels that rotated when they were stored so they were flat into a recession on the underside. When the wheels touched the ground Jean snapped a locking lever into place the secure them from folding back up. She then continued to pull the cargo box out until it reached its full length and was stopped by catches on the end towards the cab.

Sue watched from the sidewalk and as Jean stepped back she studied the structure and then said to Jean "you are right, he could patent that. I was expecting you to just lift the hard shell cover like other people, but then I thought you are not married to other people, you are married to Willie."

"Oh the cover does lift up", Jean said and to show her she inserted a key into a lock on the cover and turned it. Then she lifted the cover and inserted a prop rod into a socket to hold it in place and stepped back. The cargo drawer was incased in a liner that was about three inches smaller than the truck bed. This left room along the side for Willie to store things that he didn't want in the box. On one side Sue could see a tarp folded up and slid into the space. There was also a length of rope, a tow strap, tire chains and of course some fishing equipment. On the other side were two panels of thin plywood. Sue looked at them and Jean could see she needed to explain their use. These panels fit over the two rails that slide out before the box is pulled out. They make a nice table to use when we go on fishing trips. She then pointed into the box, which was dived into compartments, to folding chairs that had extended legs," Willie put longer legs on those so we can sit up to the end gate table and eat lunch".

Sue was still looking at the wheels on the drawer and told Jean that they reminded her of the wheels of an ambulance gurney. Jean said that's where they came from. "Willie said he got the idea when he was loaded into the ambulance after the wall fell on him. I can't imagine that if I was bloodied and bruised from an experience like that that I would be thinking about constructing something in the back of a pickup truck using wheels from the gurney I was riding on". Jean laughed as she said it; "but then we are not talking about me we are talking about Willie".

"I will have to talk to Max about helping Willie get some kind of a patent on this", Sue commented as she loaded her bags into the compartments Jean indicated." Even if it limits the use of the truck I think it is just cool enough to sell."

"Oh, Sue, this is Willie we are talking about. This whole box is in its own shell and if I push it back in and lift up on those levers on the sides the whole thing slides out. There is another set of wheels on the front end and both sets drop through slots on the bottom of the liner and it can be wheeled out of the way. Turn a couple of latches and the cover comes off and it's ready to be used for whatever you want to haul in it.

Sue just looked at the truck and said "Yup, Max has to help Willie market this".

Jean ran her hand along the smooth side of the truck and quietly said "yes that would be nice".

After loading the bags into the cargo box and Sue insisting that Jean let her close everything up the two of them turned and headed to the cab. Sue took one last look at the house and yard then turned and opened the door. She just giggled and hopped up onto the captain's chair that swiveled and reclined and was there in place of the original bench seat. She looked at Jean and Jean said "Oh, don't worry he's still got the original pieces he's removed all shoved up into the rafters of the machine shed at home".

"Let me guess", Sue said "resale, right?"

"You guessed it, like he is ever going to sell this thing, but you know boys; they get older but they never do grow up." Then the two of them laughed for several minutes. They laughed like they used to when they were young and before life's problems took the laughter from them.

When the two of then finally quit giggling Sue wiped her eyes and looked around at the interior of the pickup. The dash had a CD/AM FM radio. There were extra ports for plugging in chargers and other electronic devices, gauges for every motor function she could think of and a couple she had no idea what they were for. In the space between the seats there was a console with a magazine rack, cup holders and more plug in ports. In the roof near the windshield there was a small TV and a GPS system.

Jeans eyes followed Sues as they roamed over the interior and all of the gadgets Willie had installed. When she saw that Sue was looking at the TV and GPS she said "those two are mine, Willie insists on using a map for directions and doesn't watch much television."

"Max is the same way, he would rather read a book than watch a movie," Sue said; then she added in a fake southern belle voice, "Boys, whatever are we to do with them" as she pretended to fan herself like a character from an old movie. This started the giggles again for a while; then they both fell silent, lost in thoughts of the two men and wondering if things would work out and the past friendship could be resurrected through the layers of time that had settled over it.

Chapter 2

As Max walked down the steps Willie came to meet him, he walked quickly, but Max thought he detected a stiffness in his steps. "Probably just age," he thought as Willie extended one hand to take a bag from Max and the other hand to shake the hand he had liberated from its burden. The handshake lasted a very long time. They looked at each other with giant schoolboy grins on their faces and each of them not knowing how to start a conversation with a person they hadn't seen for a lifetime and had parted from under less than friendly terms. The awkwardness of the situation was pushed aside when they both said at the same time "Gosh it's really good to see you."

When the handshake finally ended the bags that had been set on the ground were retrieved and Max adjusted the messenger bag he carried over his shoulder. They turned and headed for the "truck".

Max followed Willie and noticed that his steps were more lively and quick than when he had approached him on the steps. They circled around to the passenger side of the cab and Willie stopped a little past the passenger door. There he lifted a handle and a small door opened to reveal a small compartment. Willie told Max this would be his "clothes dresser drawer" for the trip; and he should put ever thing he didn't need while they were driving in there. Willie then lifted the bag he had carried and slid it into the compartment, and Max did the same with the one he was carrying. The messenger bag he left hooked over his shoulder; he had never rode in a semi truck before and had brought some books and magazines along in case he got too bored. He had also brought some files of cases he was working on, but didn't really know if that had been such a good idea, especially after what Willie said next. As he handed Max a key that he said locked both the door to the cab and the side compartment door Willie told him to make sure the compartment was locked at all times and the cab was locked whenever they were out of the truck; "this is the world on the other side of the "cracks" in society that you here people falling through." Willie said this as he looked over his shoulder as if he expected someone to be trying to sneak up on him right there.

Max began to have the same doubts he had felt on the drive to the truck stop. He looked around, double checked the door to the compartment to make sure he had locked it properly and wondered if he really should have accepted Willies invitation to take a road trip to yesterday.

He looked at Willie with a look of deep concern and fear and Willie said, "don't worry so much, it really isn't that bad but I just wanted to stress the fact that it could be, and at times has been, a not so pleasant place to live.

Remember you are not in a gated community. There are no locked gates on a truck stop; even though most of them have security patrols in their lots there is nothing to stop a criminal from getting in. Just remember there were rattlesnakes in the grass when we were fishing but it never stopped us from enjoying the day. There are rattlesnakes of a different kind in this section of society but don't let that fact stop you from enjoying the adventure. Now let's get something to eat, I've been waiting for you so we can have breakfast together before we leave. I hope you haven't eaten yet."

Max said that he hadn't and the two of them turned and walked side-by-side to the restaurant in the main building of the truck stop. As they walked Max caught himself looking under the trucks they walked past. "Now he's got me looking for rattlesnakes in the truck stop," he thought. Then he smiled and thought to himself "Yea, Max old boy you ain't in Kansas anymore". Then he noticed he was lagging a little behind Willie so he stepped up his pace and walked beside his old friend into the great unknown world of trucking. As they walked Max asked Willie if the food was any good and Willie said he would have to decide that for himself. "There is a pretty good variety to choose from so you should find something you can swallow. There is a good salad bar with quite a lot of fruits and vegetables, and both of them are fairly fresh, their burgers aren't real greasy and the servers are friendly, so yea, I guess I would say it's an ok place to eat.

They entered the restaurant and Max was surprised to see that it resembled any other restaurant. The place was clean, orderly and even at this early hour was fairly busy.

Max commented to Willie about all the people up at this early hour and Willie tried to explain the daily routine of an over-the-road truck driver to him, as they seated themselves at a table in the dining section.

"Most people in the general public have a very false idea of what it is like to be a truck driver", Willie said. "They watch a movie about some bumbling police chasing a crazy truck in a race to do something or the other, and they think that's reality. The only time most of them see us is on the highway and then we are just a bother to them because of the size of the truck and the fact that it doesn't get out of the way as fast as a passenger vehicle does. The truth is that we are just people trying to do a job and raise a family. Like every other section of society there are good and bad, but for the most part we just want to get the job done and go home to our families."

Max got a little embarrassed when Willie talked about people in passenger vehicle getting impatient when they get behind a truck at a stoplight. He thought about all the times he had accelerated around a truck just to find it behind him a couple miles down the road.

Willie was talking about how much fuel it takes to get a truck rolling up to highway speed and how expensive it is to operate and make a profit. "This is a very competitive industry and an owner operator has to be a good business person to make it work. Most people think we are just a bunch of gypsies going wherever we want whenever we want, but the truth is very different. Our lives are more regulated than almost any other section of society. We are restricted to which roads we can drive on, how many hours we can drive and when we can deliver our loads. We are given a pickup time and number often before the product has even been manufactured, and at the same time we are given a time and place to deliver it. This is done by inventory clerks working in a cubicle in some office and it is up to us to make it work. The shortest and quickest routes are often not open to truck traffic because of a local ordinance or a state law restricting weights or lengths of vehicles. This is an around the clock and around the calendar industry that makes it possible for the rest of the country to keep going and growing. We are the more visible portion of the section of society that isn't strictly eight-to-five. There are a lot of people who work evening and night shifts and so do we. It's easy to overlook the fact that when you get up for work there are a lot of people already working so when you get to the gas station you can get a nice cup of coffee and a roll before work. Or that if you get sick in the middle of the night you won't have to wait until morning to see a doctor. Truck drivers are no different than any other shift worker except that we drive our office to the destination instead of our office being the destination."

Max looked at Willie and said with a smile, "I don't remember you ever talking that much when we were young." This caused Willie to blush a little as he realized he had been sort of preaching. He covered his embarrassment by picking up the menu and looking around the dining room.

When their food arrived and they began eating the awkwardness of their situation began to lessen and they began talking about their lives of the past forty years, but as they talked and Max looked around he noticed that

Willie kept glancing at a man sitting alone in a booth across the room from them. The man was wearing a black suit coat which looked like it was a couple sizes too big. He had a long thin face made longer by a full beard. The beard matched the color of his hair which was long and much uncombed. The black hair and beard were streaked with grey, or more correctly the grey hair and beard were streaked with black because grey was the dominate color. The man looked to be about in his mid fifties. He was rather thin looking with long slim fingers which held the cup of tea from which his took occasional sips. The thing Max noticed most about the man was his eyes; even from across the room they looked very dark and piercing. He also noticed that they were directed at their table; "no gates to screen who gets in and rattlesnakes in the grass," thanks again Willie, he thought. Now everyone is out to get me.

They talked and ate and when they were finished eating and just finishing the last refill of their coffee cups Willie surprised Max by saying he had to go over and talk to the very person Max was sure was some kind of spy or something. Willie got up and left Max sitting by himself," well I guess his manners haven't improved, at least he could have told me who he was or even invited me to go meet him. I wonder what the secret is." Max began to have the same troubling thoughts that had bothered him on his drive to the truck stop. What did he really know about the guy Willie had become over the last four decades? He began to think about the times he and Sue had been back to Minnesota, and realized there hadn't been that many. One thing Willie and he had in common was that neither of them had any brothers or sisters. This fact was probably the reason they were so close growing up. Max's parents had both died quite young and after they were gone and their house had been sold there just were not a lot of reasons to return to Minnesota. After the wall collapse and all the insurance claims and out of pocket costs connected to it Sue's father had never been able to rebuild his company or reputation and slid into a steep decline, dragging her mother down with him. Trying to recapture their social status they began frequenting the social hotspots too frequently until they were no longer socialites but just social drunks. Soon the damage took its toll and one night coming home from a bar they both died in a one car accident. Sue had never been real close with her two sisters and so she found no reason to return to Minnesota either.

Sue still sent cards to her sisters and to Jean, but they had become the repetition of the old line "good to hear from you; we'll have to get together some time ".

Sue was quite surprised when Jean had called her and talked about the two boys getting together for a road trip and class reunion. She had convinced Sue to convince Max that it was a good idea for the two of them to do this and patch up their old friendship. Sue's job hadn't been easy but she had finally talked him into it. Max had agreed to go along with Willie in the truck under the condition that if it didn't work he would fly home. He had often thought about contacting Willie and seeing if there was any way they could get together, but then he would think about the "stupidest thing I ever did", as he always called it when he thought about the incident with the skunk.

That thought brought him back to the present and he glanced at the booth where Willie and the stranger were still talking. The stranger glanced quickly around the room and then at Max while reaching into an inner pocket of the oversized coat he was wearing. He looked back at Willie and said something as he slid an envelope across the table to him.

Willie reached out and covered the envelope with his hand and pulled it towards him. The two of them talked for a while and then Willie stood up moving his hand and the envelope to the pocket of his jacket. As the other person also stood up Willie withdrew his hand without the envelope and shook hands with his friend, they had a few more words together and the man with the beard turned and left the restaurant. Again Max wondered if he really knew the man approaching his table from across the room... He wondered what Willie had been involved in over the past decades. Willie had said himself that there were a lot of snakes in his world; could it be that it was personal experience that made him say that?

When Willie returned to the table he apologized for leaving so suddenly. He must have noticed the concerned look on Max's face because he said "relax the guys harmless." Then he went on to explain the meeting and the stranger with the long beard.

According to Willie the guy that had Max wondering if he should just trust his instincts and forget about going on this road trip with him was a professor at one of the colleges in southern California. When Max asked which one Willie got a little evasive and said he wasn't sure. He said he hasn't known the guy very long and that was just what he had told him. Willie said he has a slightly Middle Eastern accent but says he's a U.S. citizen. Willie had only met him a couple months earlier in the restaurant while he was in the line for the buffet. After that first meeting the guy had seemed to be at the restaurant every time he stopped and would always strike up a conversation with him and sit at his table while they ate.

Willie said the guy was really interesting to talk to because he had a very good understanding of what was going on in the world. Willie asked Max if he was aware of the fact that when the Iraq war started one of the first buildings to be ransacked and almost destroyed was the cultural building of antiquities. Max admitted that he was not a big listener of the news, neither local nor world, and Willie said that was what most people said that he talked to about the subject. Willie talked about what the man had said about the looting of the cultural building, and about the treasures that had been stolen and lost forever. The guy said the Middle East was his favorite area of study and that he had a list of the items that had been looted from the museum. He talked about the Middle East being the cradle of civilization and that some of the items stolen were over five thousand years old. "Actually he was always talking, and I did a lot of listening," Willie said. "I listened because he always bought breakfast; small price to pay for listening right," Willie said. Then he flashed that twinkle eyed smile that Max remembered so well.

"He says he has a small crate that he would like me to deliver; well actually there are two small crates that he wants me to deliver to some people in Minnesota. He paid pretty well so I said I would do It. He says they are from the college he works for, but I don't really believe him, and I don't really care. The money he just paid me is more that the whole load of produce I'm taking back. He said all I have to do is deliver my produce and there would be someone there to pick up the crates. No questions asked."

That last statement started Max thinking about rattle snakes again, "Yea there will probably be someone there to pick up the packages and us too "He thought. Then he started thinking about getting up and telling Willie he didn't think this trip was such a good idea, but he held his tongue and didn't say anything. He thought maybe Willie's business wasn't doing very good and that is why he would do business with the rattlesnakes that he had warned him about.

After another cup of coffee and a final trip to the bathroom Willie put some money on the table and said it was time to load and get this adventure underway.

Max had thought about calling Sue but had decided that it was too early and didn't want to wake her. Now as he followed Willie out of the restaurant to the truck he wondered when he would get to talk to her again. He caught himself looking around expecting to see guys with turbans on their heads or men with dark glasses following them, but all he saw were "t" shirts, blue jeans and work boots; and a blur of faces none of them having beards.

The two of them walked together to the rear of the trailer and Willie opened the swinging doors. As light flooded into the interior it showed an almost empty space. Almost empty because in the front of the trailer against the front wall there were two small wooden crates about two feet long, one foot wide and one foot high. They had been secured in place by a ratcheting bar known as a load lock. Willie was satisfied that they would ride without moving around so he just closed the door without saying a word.

As Willie closed the door Max looked around to see if there was anyone watching them but he couldn't see anyone acting suspicious and he turned to Willie and asked;" What's in the crates?" Willie looked at him and said quietly, "I don't know, but I hope it's legal." After securing the latches and putting a paddle lock on the left door he said to Max it was time to go and headed up the left side of the trailer to the cab of the truck. Max started walking up the right side and again caught himself looking for rattlesnakes under the trailer and ninja warriors attacking from behind.

After they had both entered the cab and put on their seatbelts Willie started the engine and while it was warming up and the air pressure was building up he explained the loading process to Max. "First we go to a farm about ten miles from here to pick up oranges. We only get about a third of the load there. The next stop is about fifty miles from the first pickup where we get the rest of the order, which is grapefruit and lemons." As he was talking Max was only half listening. He was totally surprised at the view from the cab of the semi. This was the first time he had ever been in a truck this size and it was a little frightening to be seated that far above the ground. As he adjusted his seat and got settled in he felt a little more comfortable, but grabbed the door handle when Willie released the parking brake and began backing out of the parking space. Willie was still talking about the loading process. "After we get the second pickup on the trailer we can start heading east. Hopefully we can get loaded without too much trouble."

"What kind of trouble are you talking about?" Max asked, with a hint of alarm in his voice; still thinking about the bearded guy.

"Oh, just the usual, workers deciding they don't want to work, the weather not cooperating with the harvest, a long line of trucks ahead of us waiting for their orders, mechanical breakdowns." "Ok, I get the picture. I was just thinking about other trouble." Max glanced at Willie who was concentrating on maneuvering the truck out of the lot, he thought he noticed a slight grin on his face but decided it was just that Willie was happy to finally be moving towards home. Max on the other hand was still thinking about those mysterious crates in the trailer and rattlesnakes.

Just as he began to relax a little the refrigeration unit on the trailer burst into life with a loud roar. Max jumped and Willie laughed. "Relax, it's just the refer kicking in to pre-cool the trailer. The trailer has to be at the temperature the shippers require before they will load us. So I turned it on when I walked past it to get into the cab. It will run until it reaches the temperature that it's set for then it will shut down. Once we get loaded the refer will have to run constantly to eliminate moisture that builds up from the produce sweating. If the moisture isn't removed the boxes will get wet and the constant rubbing together while we drive will wear the outer surface of the boxes off, then the buyer will call it damaged goods and refuse to pay full price for the load. The product is still good and the stores don't display the product in the boxes but they still get away with charging the trucking company for damage. So it's cheaper for me to pay for extra fuel than it is to pay for wet containers."

Willie had the truck out of the parking space and was about to start out of the lot when he turned to Max and asked if there was anything he might have left in his car because if there was now would be the time to remember it.

"No, I'm pretty sure I have everything I need," Max said, but to himself he said, I know a good lawyer which is probably the one thing I'm going to need most, as he thought about the strange twist his normally mundane life had just taken in the past couple hours.

"Alright then, its showtime," Willie said as he pulled out of the parking lot and down the street to enter the fast moving stream of traffic on the interstate.

As Willie guided the truck through traffic Max was busy trying to adjust to being so high above the road surface. Willie glanced at him laughed and said, "You haven't ridden in a truck before have you?" Max said he hadn't and asked if it was that obvious. Willie laughed again and said it was because every time they went under an overpass Max would duck his head. "It's a little different being this close to them isn't it?" He said to Max as they went under another overpass.

Max agreed that the perspective from the cab of a truck was quite different but that it was nice to see beyond the guardrail, which in a car is at eye level and blocks most of the view.

"I like to think of the cab of my truck as my mobile office and the windshield as an ever changing screensaver. My office doesn't contain a supervisor looking over my shoulder but I am still being watched very closely. The companies on both ends of my trip are watching through their inventory charts where every orange or whatever it is I'm hauling is at any given moment. They both use trucks as part of their warehousing. Neither one enters product in route into their books as inventory buy they both count it as theirs. It saves them money to have product housed in trailers on the road but they have to make sure that product will be in their warehouse when they need it to sell to their customers. They calculate when they will need a product and send an order out and set up a delivery time usually before the product has been produced or harvested. With produce, as soon as it is picked from a tree dug from the ground or pulled off a vine the shelf-life clock is ticking down. Consumers have been programmed to only buy the very best looking product and that means the freshest product. They pay a high price for good looking food and it is up to the trucks to deliver it to them.

Max was listening to Willie but he couldn't get the thoughts of the guy in the restaurant and the two crates in the trailer they were pulling out of his mind.

His attention was drawn to a sport-utility vehicle that had been moving along in front of them but now seemed to be slowing down. The windows were tinted preventing him from actually seeing the occupants but he could see their forms and it was obvious that the passenger was turning around and looking at them. He wondered why Willie didn't just change lanes and go around the vehicle and glanced over to see Willie straighten up in his seat and glance nervously from one mirror to the other. "What's going on?" he asked a little panicked by the action of the sport utility vehicle. "Why don't you pass those guys?"

"I can't pass, there's a vehicle right beside us that is just sitting there going the same speed as we are; I've slowed down and now he has slowed down."

"What do they want?" Max asked; now very excited.

"I don't know, I thought they were some friends of yours seeing you off on the trip. You're the one who lives out here not me." Willie said.

"Yes, but I'm not the one who took money from someone I barely knew to transport something across the country when I didn't even ask what I was to transport." Max was getting upset, but calmed down a little when the vehicle in front of them suddenly accelerated and disappeared into the traffic and the vehicle beside them switched lanes and exited the freeway.

Willie looked a Max and said he shouldn't be so nervous. "It's only traffic."

The rest of the trip to the produce farm was uneventful and as Willie turned off the secondary road they were on and drove up a paved driveway to the pickup warehouse Max stared in amazement.

When Willie had said they were going to pick up at a farm the mental picture Max had formed was the small family farms he remembered from his childhood in Minnesota. This place did not fit his description of a farm. It was huge, with large buildings equipped with huge cooling fans and refrigeration units on them. Dozens of trucks pulling refrigerated trailers waiting to be loaded.

There were rows of farm machinery parked and dozens of small trucks loaded with oranges waiting to unload them into the warehouse. Some trucks were parked under conveyors that dumped oranges into them. When those trucks were full they disappeared around the buildings and another took its place under the conveyor.

Willie guided his truck skillfully through a maze of machinery and pulled up behind the last truck in a line formed along the wall of a building with a sign reading shipping. "Shouldn't have had that last cup of coffee," Willie said as he retrieved a paper from his briefcase. "It might be a long wait if all these trucks have to be loaded before us. Some warehouses work on a first come first served basis regardless what the order says the pickup time is. Others work by appointment only; let's hope this is one of those because my appointment time is fifteen minutes from now.

Willie opened his door and told Max to follow him as he headed for a door marked driver check-in. As Max started to follow Max he remembered he hadn't locked the door and turned around took his key and locked it from the outside. When he turned back Willie had already disappeared through the door and he hurried to catch up. When he entered the building he saw Willie crossing the warehouse floor heading towards an enclosed office with a sliding glass window, through which he could see a dozen people moving around from file cabinets to desks to other windows along the wall; with other people standing at them. Willie stood by the window for a short time and a hand suddenly appeared from below the counter, on the other side and slid the window open. Then a voice called out "pickup number". Willie read off his number from the paper he had taken out of his briefcase. The hand appeared again and slid the window closed then disappeared. Willie stood there and said nothing but Max edged closer to see who was attached to the mysterious hand. He looked in the window to see a guy busily sorting through a stack of papers in front of him. About half way through the stack he pulled one out and reached up, slid the window open handed the paper to Willie and said "door three." His hand reached up and slid the window closed and he went back to the stack of papers on his desk all without looking up.

Willie wrote three on his paper and said they lucked out because this place goes by appointment.

They walked back to the truck and went to the back of the trailer where Willie undid the lock and opened the swinging doors. Max was looking into the trailer as light flooded in and again shown on the two crates secured against the front wall of the trailer. As was becoming somewhat of a habit he turned around expecting to see a group of men approaching from behind one of the other trucks. There were no shady characters only trucks waiting to load or unload oranges, warehouse workers on forklifts, and rows of machinery waiting for someone to start them up to accomplish whatever they were designed to accomplish.

"You going to stand there looking like a tourist, or are you going to ride along?" Willies comment brought him back from his thoughts and Max walked quickly up the side of the trailer to the cab of the truck and he unlocked the door and climbed up into the seat.

"I sure am glad we don't have to wait for all those other trucks to get loaded ahead of us. We would be here all day." Willie was talking as they walked towards the service door near the dock door they had just backed up to.

The service door led into the warehouse and although it was still quite early the temperature was already starting to climb. Max was thinking that the new blue jeans would be getting uncomfortable but when the stepped into the building he was glad he had them on; in fact he wished he would have grabbed his light jacket from beside his seat in the truck. The warehouse was a giant refrigerator and was kept around forty degrees, which was an abrupt change from the humidity and heat outside. As they walked to the door marked with a number three painted on the floor Max commented that he was glad they weren't picking up frozen product.

When they arrived at the door Willie took hold of a metal ring in a depression on a metal plate and pulled. The ring was attached to a chain and this was evidently attached to some kind of a spring under the plate because the whole thing came up forming a ramp which Willie walked up causing it to move downward. At the same time a lip on the outer edge of the ramp began moving up so that when the ramp was again at floor level there was a lip extending into the trailer forming a bridge over the space between it and the dock wall. After this move Willie stood to the side of the ramp inside a square marked with yellow lines.

He indicated to Max that he should also stand inside the square, saying that if they didn't stay in the square they wouldn't get loaded. "They don't want people wandering around the warehouse floor when there are forklifts working; it's a commonsense thing because they wouldn't get much done if they had to constantly stop for someone to walk in front of them. And also it is hard to see beyond a pallet that is taller than they are.

They stood by the door for awhile and it soon became very apparent to Max why it was important that the forklift operators knew exactly where the drivers were. There were over two dozen lift trucks operating on the warehouse floor at the same time doing the job of loading trucks, unloading trucks, retrieving pallets from cold storage bins and moving pallets into cold storage bins. The whole operation was like a choreographed symphony. And like an opera the performers didn't need the audience wandering around the stage.

After a few minutes one of the lift truck operators wheeled up to their door and stopped in front of them. Willie handed him the paper he was holding and the guy punched some keys on an onboard electronic locator handed the paper back to Willie and wheeled away; all without saying a word.

After another short wait the driver returned with a pallet of oranges. He pulled up and looked into the trailer and asked Willie what he wanted to do with the two cases already in the trailer. Willie said that the pallet of oranges should fit beside them and he wanted to leave them where they were if he could.

The lift operator said he didn't see a problem with that and rolled into the trailer, returning a short time later without the pallet. The forklift made thirteen more trips into and out of the trailer, and after the last trip the driver stopped beside them and handed Willie a clipboard with a paper on it that the driver had been marking down the pallet numbers as he loaded them into the trailer; Willie signed the paper and handed it back to the driver. They were then instructed to go back to the window they had checked in at. As they left the lift operator punched keys on the locator keyboard, put the clipboard down and was gone to another truck at another door.

After receiving their shipping papers they returned to the dock door and Willie walked into the trailer to install load locks behind the last two pallets to prevent them from tipping over. He then reset the dock plate pulled the overhead door down and headed for the service door. "That guy sure doesn't talk much," Max said as they walked.

"That's good, some guys talk more than they work and it takes forever to get loaded," Willie said as he opened the door and they were hit with a blast of hot humid air from the outside.

After pulling a short distance away from the dock Willie stopped the truck and got out, walked to the rear of the trailer and closed and secured the doors.

As they drove out to the main road Willie turned to Max and said he must be good luck because he had never gotten loaded that fast before, "I hope the second pick goes that fast, because then we will be ahead of schedule and that is a good thing."

The next pickup went just as smooth as the first one. The fifty miles they drove to get there had been incident free and Max was starting to relax. When they arrived the person behind the glass window had directed them around some other trucks to a dock where they went through the same procedure as they had at the first warehouse. Opening the overhead door then setting the dock plate and waiting in the yellow square for a lift truck operator to load them. They picked up six pallets of grapefruit and two pallets of lemons. The trailer was now full and Willie secured the last pallets with his locks which he had removed when they arrived. They went to the sliding glass window and received their paper work and headed for the service door where they were greeted with another blast of hot humid air.

In the cab of the truck Willie slipped the paperwork into a battered folder and put it into a pouch on the inside of the driver's door. After pulling ahead and securing the trailer doors he seated himself in his seat drew a couple lines in his logbook and said "well are you ready to go to Minnesota?"

Max had not thought about that part of the trip since the parking lot when he had arrived at the truck stop. Things had been happening so fast, and the events were so different from his normal routine that Max had not really had time to sort them out and put them into a proper sequence. Years of working as a lawyer had trained him to always sort events out and categorize them for future use. The events of the past few hours required an entire restructuring of his mental filing system, because he had no other experiences to compare them to. He had no files in his experience for shady looking characters with beards, mysterious crates with unknown contents, Factory farms or vehicles blocking him on the road for no reason he could see.

He told Willie he was as ready as he would ever be as he glanced out the window looking for something familiar in this strange new section of society that he found himself in.

The only familiar thing he found was Willie; and he wasn't sure he really knew the guy in the seat next to him anymore.

While Willie maneuvered the truck out of the driveway of the farm, Max tried to adjust the seat trying to get as comfortable as possible for what he knew was going to be a very long ride. Making small talk he asked Willie how his life had been over the past decades. He was thinking about the two crates in the trailer and the envelope in Willies pocket. He had some concern that maybe Willie was in financial trouble, but didn't want to embarrass him by asking him outright.

Willie looked over at Max, glanced in the passenger side mirror, back at the driver's side mirror, scanned the gauges on the dash and leaned back in the seat.

"Oh, it's been a pretty good life," he said. "I've been able to raise the kids, fix up the house and put a few dollars in the bank." He gestured towards a picture on the dash that Max had noticed when he got in the first time but hadn't paid much attention to. The picture was one of Willie and Jean standing in front of a very nice house with their children.

"You don't even recognize the old shack, do you?" As realization set in, Max was amazed that the house was the small farmhouse Willie had grown up in, but with upgrades.

"Wow," was all Max could say when he recognized what he was looking at. "You really did some big changes on that place."

"Yea, Jean and the kids helped me with a lot of it, but we hired the main construction work done. It's really comfortable, and there's a lot more room than we need now that the kids are gone. The house was never insulated that well and the windows leaked but it is pretty sung and warm now. I always kid Jean that her and her next husband will be happy there after she works me to death." Willie looked at the picture with a smile on his lips but when Max looked closely at him he thought he detected a look of deep sadness in his eyes. But before he could dwell on it Willie said "hey, did you notice the far right of the photo?"

Max had been concentrating on the house and the people in the picture and hadn't looked at the rest of it. Now as his vision shifted and expanded he saw something that made his heart shrink and a flood of memories rushed into his thoughts.

Like a dam bursting all the memories, fears and regrets of the past forty years came flooding back in and foremost of those memories was the one that caused him the greatest anguish; the one incident he has regretted since the day it happened.

On the far right edge of the photo was an ugly green-yellow or yellow-green international pickup truck, parked next to a neatly painted garden shed. It was the same garden shed he remembered Willie going into to get the fork to dig worms; the same one he had went to when he returned Willie's bait worms to the garden after the incident with the wall. And that was the same pickup that Max had been trying to forget about for the past four decades.

He was sure now that Willie still thought about the prank that he had pulled on him. The prank that was conceived by his football buddies who urged him to do it. The same guys who denied having anything to do with it, and had shunned Max after it happened. Max had lost his one good friend because of his guilt and the "friends" on the football team deserted him, so he only had Sue left to talk with and she was not very kind to him for awhile either. She had told him how stupid he was for listening to the other players, and going along with them in this childish prank to humiliate his friend. Although she was upset with him she was still in love with him and had not deserted him like the rest of them. She stuck with him in his dream of becoming a lawyer and married him soon after high school. She was still with him, his best and closest friend, the most important part of his life; and now that ugly pickup was back in his life; if only in a photo. She had moved to California with him and worked to pay the bills he couldn't cover while he went to school. Now she had encouraged him to take this trip and he wondered why. He looked at the photo and cautiously looked at Willie but could see no indication that he was even thinking of the incident or revenge, or that he was involved with a sinister organization shipping crates of contraband across the country in produce trailers. All he saw was Willie beaming like a school boy with his first "A" on his report card.

"I'll bet you never thought I would still have that old truck," he said. "I've overhauled and remodeled that as much as I have the house. Updated it with a lot of modern systems in it including air conditioning so I don't have to have the windows open when I drive on those dusty gravel roads to go fishing

Max just stared at the truck in the photo wondering how he had missed it before. The lawyer side of him started to analyze the possibilities; had Willie switched photos for some reason when he wasn't in the seat when they stopped at a rest area a little while ago? Maybe something had moved on the dash that had been covering part of the frame, but there was nothing around it that could have shifted. If Willie switched photos, why? Was he planning to torment him all the way to Minnesota? Max began thinking again about the things that had been happening and wondered if Willie was in trouble and had decided to take Max with him if he got caught. The strange guy in the restaurant, the two vehicles slowing down in front and beside them on the highway; these thoughts kept eating at his feelings. Now added to this was a strange click in the phone every time he called Sue. He began thinking that someone was tapping his phone and wondered what he had gotten himself into. Now the appearance of the pickup truck made him think Willie was indeed playing some elaborate joke on him.

"I can't figure out why I hadn't seen the truck before," he decided to just come out and ask for an explanation.

"Oh, that's because the frame was hiding it when you were in the bunk just now to get a soda out of the fridge I shifted the picture in the frame to show the truck. The picture was about the house finally being finished, and about the family. The truck just got in it by mistake, not that Jean believed that. She was sure I posed in the right spot to include the truck. She made us do the photo over when she saw the pickup in the first one. Not that she hates the truck or anything, she just calls it my other woman and says I spend more time with that than I do with her; but she loves it when we go fishing because I've put a lot of things on it to make it quite comfortable for her. Incidentally she says the same thing about this truck we are riding in now.

Willie's explanation made sense and eased some of the tension he was feeling. He wanted to come out and ask Willie about the skunk and whether he is still harboring any resentment towards him about it, he wanted to but he didn't because just then Willie sat up straighter in his seat, buckled his seatbelt, and began checking his mirrors and slowing down.

"I can't believe this, this scale is never open when I come through here. I wonder why it is open now, this late in the day." Willie slowed down to the posted thirty miles an hour for the exit ramp to the weigh station scales and began to exit the highway. He told Max he had better get into the bunk area of the truck and close the curtain so nobody saw him.

"I didn't think we would be crossing any scales on the trip so I didn't bother getting a rider permit from the insurance company. If they start checking paperwork it might cause a problem."

"I always take this route because it cuts off a few miles and it gets me around the big scales on the interstate."

Willie was talking to Max through the curtain separating the bunk area from the rest of the cab as he slowly approached the scales. He had told Max that there was a small truck stop on this highway that he liked to stop at because it was a lot quieter than the ones on the interstate. The truck stop had a good restaurant and a motel where Max could get a room for the night because the truck only had a single bunk bed. Max had suggested that they get a room with two beds so Willie wouldn't have to sleep in the truck but he had said he was so used to sleeping in the truck when it was loaded he wouldn't be able to get to sleep in a hotel room because he would worry about the produce in the trailer. Max wondered if it was just the produce he was worried about.

Now Max was worrying about other things. He had noticed the sign indicating that the scale was open had switched to closed just as they passed it and this made Max wonder if someone had been waiting for them to drive by the scale.

Willie had told Max that they were a little later getting started and in order to get to the truck stop he might have to drive a little longer than he was supposed to. As Willie drove slowly towards the scale Max could see him glancing at his log book trying to figure out if he was over hours and if there was any way he could adjust it to make it legal. He rolled down his window to listen to the instructions from the loud speaker and looked straight ahead as he rolled onto the scale. It was after dark and the approach to the scale was lit by overhead lights that flicked on as they approached and flicked off as they passed them. The scale house itself was lit with a subdued red light and the transparent shades covering the windows gave the interior a sinister look. Max was looking through a crack in the curtain of the bunk as Willie came to a stop on the scale platform. They sat for what seemed to Max a very long time with nothing happening. Then a loud voice in the otherwise complete silence told Willie to set the brakes on the truck and not to move and someone would be out to get all the paperwork, including load sheets, drivers license, vehicle permits and proof of insurance.

When Willie opened the door for the man standing beside the truck Max could see he was a very large man with a gun strapped on his hip and a badge, that shone in the semi-darkness, pinned to his shirt. Without saying a word he reached up and took the papers that Willie handed him, turned and walked back into the small scale house. Max could barely make out movement inside the building as the man with the gun entered and sat down at a desk with the papers Willie had handed him. After looking at the papers for a few minutes he got up and walked to the console at the window picked up the microphone and as he raised it to speak the speaker on the side of the building crackled; then a voice said "please move your truck to the parking area and come inside." Then there was silence as he set the microphone down and returned to his desk.

Willie closed the door glanced back at the bunk and said, "This is not normal; I don't know what is going on, but in case you haven't noticed we are the only truck that was pulled into the scale."

Max was very nervous as he sat out of sight in the darkened bunk of the truck. He was sure they would be surrounded by gun tooting marshals and S.W.A.T. vehicles as soon as they stopped in the empty parking lot.

"I don't know how long this is going to take but stay in the bunk and feel free to stretch out on the bed if it gets to be too long." Willie was talking as he drove the truck off the scale and maneuvered it around to the parking lot. He stopped a short distance from the scale house and set the brakes. It was warm out so he shut off the engine and turned off the lights leaving Max in darkness in the bunk. The sensor activated lights in the parking lot had turned on as the motion of the vehicle set them off but now there was no movement and they shut off one by one until the lot was once again in darkness.

Willie sat for a couple seconds in the seat then said "well here goes nothing". He opened the door and the cab light flicked on causing the nearest overhead light in the lot to turn on. Max watched Willie walk towards the building then he glanced out the passenger side window through a crack in the curtain. He was sure there would be a sudden charge of police vehicles from behind the large building on the opposite side of the parking lot; but there was no movement that he could see. The overhead light that had turned on when Willie opened his door barely lit the building and all he saw just before it shut off was a sliver of metal sticking out from the far side of the building. He assumed it was a highway warning sign; one of those high visibility lime-green signs they put up in construction zones. Before he could study it for long the overhead light flicked off and he was once again in darkness. There was not even the red glow from the scale-house to give a little light to the darkness. This side of the building was windowless and after Willie closed the service door there was no light at all.

When the last light went out Max leaned back and rested against the rear wall of the bunk. Willie had warned him against turning on any lights because of the fact he had not gotten a rider permit from his insurance company. He couldn't tell them he was a hitchhiker because most states have laws against that and he would still need a rider permit, so Max sat in the dark. He sat still not wanting to move in case someone was watching the truck. He sat in the dark and wondered how long this was going to take and if Willie would be able to talk his way clear so they could get to the truck-stop and he could get to a hotel room and away from the truck for awhile.

As Max sat in the dark bunk he listened to the traffic on the highway and wondered what had caused them to be singled out to be pulled into the scale. The sign had switched to closed as they entered and had not been turned on to open after they had entered. Why had the scale been open when Willie said that it was never open when he has been through here before? He thought about all the things that had happened during the day; starting with the guy in the restaurant and now ending the day stopped at a weigh station that was never open. He sat still for what seemed like an eternity and finally decided to move enough to check his watch, thankful that he had a button to light up the dial. He slowly pushed his sleeve up and pressed the button sure that it had been at least an hour; but the watch told him it had only been less than thirty minutes.

He sat for a little while longer and then decided to stand up and open the curtain a little, convinced that there were no mounted horsemen lurking in the darkness waiting for a reason to attack the truck. He slowly stood and with both hands separated the two halves of the curtain. After nothing happened he stuck his head out and glanced from side to side. Now that his eyes had become accustomed to the darkness he could see a little of the surrounding lot and buildings. He noticed that there was a window on this side of the scale-house but that it was dark. He also noticed that the scale itself was still lit by the red glow from the window of the room the large man with the gun had entered after taking the paperwork from Willie.

He thought about that large black man with the starched and pressed uniform and the large gun, who had stood beside the truck and took the papers from Willie. He wondered if Willie was having any luck talking his way out of whatever he had gotten himself into. He also thought about how stupid Willie was for taking money to transport something across the country for someone he barely knew. He began running a series of scenarios through his mind about what could possibly be happening in the scale-house and what the possible outcome could be for each of them, and they all ended with jail time.

He wanted to call Sue and talk to her for the comfort of her support, but decided that talking would be heard if there was anyone outside the truck. He sat for a few more minutes and then decided that if all the curtains were securely fastened and the window covers were in place that he could turn on one of the small reading lights beside the bed without drawing attention to the truck. Sitting in the dark was wearing on his nerves and he also had to go to the bathroom and could not find the port-a-potty in the dark.

Cautiously he moved back from the curtain and slid his hand very slowly and quietly from top to bottom closing the zipper and making sure the bottom was fastened securely. He then used the dial of his watch to check the windows, making sure the curtains were completely fastened by the Velcro strips. Then he turned on a small light over the desk by the head of the bed. With this small light he was able to find the port-a-potty and relieve himself. This made him feel better and he relaxed a little and began to look around what Willie called the "living room".

The desk was a small cabinet behind the passenger seat about eighteen inches wide and eighteen inches deep. It stood about twenty four inches tall with a small drawer and an open space below. The open space was covered by a curtain and this is where Willie stored the port-a-potty. Above the desk was a small corkboard bulletin board with a wooden frame. On the bulletin board held in place with colored tacks there were a few pictures, business cards and some other papers; all held in place with a tack in each corner.

One of the items on the board caught his eye and he leaned closer to read what was written on it. There were hand drawn flowers in the four corners and in capital letters across the top was written "MEMBER OF THE LIARS CLUB OF TEXAS". Below this it read, this is presented to Willie on this fourth day of July nineteen hundred and seventy four at this impromptu meeting of the newly formed liars club of greater Texas with me Bill, the self appointed president doing the presenting. This award is given to Willie whose story not even I can top. There was a signature on the bottom and the whole thing was written on a table napkin. Max thought it would make good conversation in jail if they were in the same cell after the police showed up at the weigh station, which he was still convinced was about to happen at any time. This thought brought him back to the present and he began wondering again what the reason for this situation was. He again wondered what was in the trailer besides produce.

Max tried to remember what Willie had said about the guy in the restaurant. So much had happened in such a short time that was not in his normal routine that a lot of it was still jumbled up in his mind and hadn't been sorted into orderly files like he did with everything in his memory. Willie had said that the guy was a professor at a California college but didn't know which one. He said he had talked to him several times but that he didn't know his last name. He said the guy was always talking about the Middle East and about the looting of the Bagdad museum when the American led invasion had started. He said the guy told him that a lot of the very old antiques had not been recovered and that the international police were searching and investigating all over the world for them. Max wondered which objects had not been recovered and if they would fit into small crates; he also wondered who the international police were. He wondered if they had any authority in the middle of Wyoming. Was there really an organization called the international police? These thoughts combined with the already confusing mass of information he had received during the day caused Max to again question the decision to take this trip.

Max thought about how happy and ordered his life was before Willie had called and proposed this insane trip. He still couldn't figure out why he had agreed to go along in the first place. Sue had kept telling him that he should do it because he talked about Willie often and she thought it would be a chance to reconnect with the two people they still thought about from Minnesota.

It was true that he had thought about Willie over the past years and had on occasion thought about calling, but had never followed through with those ideas. The years had passed and it turned out to be Willie who had made the call, and now Max was sitting in the bunk of a semi truck in a weigh station in the middle of Wyoming waiting for the international police to arrest him for smuggling stolen contraband across state lines.

After what seemed like an eternity, but was less than an hour Willie showed up at the driver's door of the truck; just Willie, no S.W.A.T., no mounted riders waving rifles and no international police. He opened the door and climbed up into the driver's seat.

"Well, that was interesting, the authorities had decided to do a spot check on trucks that passed this scale and they just happened to pick us," Willie talked as he started the engine and began moving towards the exit of the parking lot. "They asked me how often I use this route and why I didn't take the interstate. They checked all the paperwork and then told me to have a good night. They even said it would be alright for me to drive to the truck stop even though I'm out of driving time on my logbook. They said it was their fault and I agreed."

Max stayed in the bunk until they were on the highway and well away from the weigh station. Then he opened the curtain and got into the passenger seat. "You mean to tell me that whole thing was just an unfortunate luck of the draw mishap?" Max found it hard to believe Willie's story but Willie insisted that it was exactly that.

Willie was driving a little slower than he had been before the weigh station incident and Max thought he looked a little pale and like he was in some pain. Max questioned him about it but he just said he was ready for the day to end and get some sleep.

Before they had reached the weigh station Willie was telling Max that the truck stop he planned to stop at was just a little ways down the road and now both of them were eager to get there to get out of the truck and relax for the night.

The lights of the truck stop finally appeared and the two of them relaxed a little knowing that the end of this strange day was getting close. The day had been strange for Max but for Willie it had been quite routine, except that he had a passenger in his truck; something that was a little strange for him because he was used to driving alone.

As Willie maneuvered the truck and trailer through a maze of vehicles first to the fuel pumps and then to a parking space that put them as close to the hotel as they could get, Max wondered how the system ever worked. All he saw seemed like mass confusion but Willie said he saw one of the greatest achievements of the modern world. The distribution system of the United States was the greatest thing ever conceived. It combined the genius of the German interstate road system with the great American free enterprise system to build the world's greatest economy. Anything a person wanted and could afford could be purchased and delivered overnight. All of it moved by trucks. Max had mentioned that a lot of merchandise was shipped by rail and Willie had just said that there were no train tracks through the parking lot of any mall. There were trucks at both ends of a railroad to move the freight to and from the rail yard. Nothing arrived anywhere that hadn't been on a truck at some point in its delivery. People loved them, and people hated them, but the truth was that people needed them. After Willies sermon Max still only saw confusion on eighteen wheels.

When Willie finally set the parking brake and turned off the engine they both leaned back in their seats and let the days troubles drain out of them. They both felt like they had just finished a marathon race and as the stress of the day drained away they both sat in their seats and stared vacantly through the windshield, lost in their own thoughts.

After a few minutes of daydreaming Willie asked if Max wanted to get something to eat or if he just wanted to check into the room at the hotel and wait until morning to eat.

Max said he just wanted to shower and go to bed. He asked Willie again if he was sure he didn't want to share a room with him, but Willie said he would be more comfortable in the truck where he could make sure that it was secure and the reefer didn't quit running for some reason. He said he had heard about drivers that had lost their entire load because they had been in a hotel room and someone had shut their reefer unit off because they didn't like the noise. He said he didn't know if it was true but he wasn't going to take the chance of it happening to him.

They sat for a few more minutes before either of them made an attempt to move. As they sat looking at the activity in the parking lot around them Max glanced at Willie who had been acting a little different since the stop at the weigh station. Max couldn't tell if it was pain, sadness, worry or a combination of the three, but something was slightly different in his actions. Max wondered what had really gone on in the darkened room with the big man with the gun.

As he retrieved his bag from the side compartment of the truck and headed towards the hotel he decided that Willie was just tired and that having a passenger had changed his routine as much as being one had change his. Max decided that if he had disrupted Willies routine it was a good thing because Willie had sure disrupted his with this whole, "let's get together for a trip to Minnesota" thing. Returning to the present when he arrived at the hotel he put thoughts of gangsters, crooks and rattlesnakes in the parking lot out of his head and replaced them with thoughts of a soothing shower and a comfortable bed. He went through the process of checking in and finding his room and dropped his bag on the bed and his body into a padded chair and just sat there.

After Max had finally roused himself off the chair, showered, called Sue and ate a sandwich he ordered from room service he turned off the lights to go to bed; but before he got under the covers he went to the window and opened the curtains slightly. He looked out at the sea of trucks illuminated by the parking lot lights. As he looked out trying to figure out which direction he was facing he realized he was on the same side of the building they had parked on and that Willies truck was directly in front of the window. The cab of the truck was facing the building and as Max looked out through the partially opened curtain he could make out a figure that turned out to be Willie. He was sitting in his lawn chair beside the cab of his truck talking to another man who was seated on the driver's side step of the truck. He watched for awhile and saw Willie gesture towards the cab of the truck. The man on the steps stood up and turned to look at the truck then looked back at Willie. They spook a while longer and then Willie reached into his pocket and took out what Max assumed to be his wallet, although at this distance he couldn't be sure. Willie handed the other man what Max figured was some money and they shook hands as if sealing some deal they had just made. After the hand shake Willie got up folded his chair and put it into the side compartment on the driver's side of the truck and climbed into the cab. Even at this distance it was clear to Max that Willie moved with a stiffness that was more noticeable than the slight sluggishness he had noticed that morning when he watched Willie climb down from his truck cab. Oh, well he thought, I guess neither one of us is as young as we used to be, and with that thought he closed the curtain and found the bed in the dark and crawled in.

It was late in the morning when Willie called Max and told him to meet him in the restaurant and Max was concerned that maybe something was wrong causing them to get such a late start; but Willie said it wasn't his idea but that he had to follow the hours of service rules that told him how long he had to stop before he could drive again. He tried to explain the rules but soon gave up and said it was the government so it's got to be complicated.

Max noticed when they met in the restaurant that Willie was acting more like he had the previous morning and decided that he was right and that the change in his routine of having him along had just tired him out.

They ate a big breakfast and while they were finishing their coffee Max looked at Willie and said, "I didn't know you were a liar."

Willie blinked and sat his coffee down and asked him what in the world he was talking about.

Max apologized for intruding on his privacy and told him about looking at the bulletin board and reading the certificate on the napkin. He apologized again for looking into his private things, but said it was hanging in plain sight and that there hadn't been a lot of things to do while he had been held prisoner in the bunk.

Willie laughed and said he accepted his apology and that it wasn't needed, because like he said the napkin was hanging in plain sight. As for the being a prisoner Willie reminded him that he hadn't been the warden but that he had been a fellow prisoner.

"That certificate was a shining moment in my not so illustrious career. When I first started trucking for a living I didn't have any contacts so I had to take loads whenever and wherever I could get them. I now have this route from Minnesota to California and right back to Minnesota, but it wasn't always that easy. I took a load to Texas at the end of June one year and ended up sitting there over the Fourth of July holiday because I couldn't find a load out the state. I got to know a couple other drivers who were stuck there also and one day we were talking about how Texans like to boast about how everything is bigger in Texas and their stories are not lies but an exaggeration of the truth. Well, I told them a true story that not even they could top."

"It was a true story about my brother and I, and how we invented Beef Jerky."

"It can't be true because you don't have a brother," Max said.

"That's right," said Willie "It's true that it is just a story, so that makes it a true story".

Max just smiled and said," With that kind of logic you could be a lawyer."

"Well, these two guys took it as a kind of personal insult that a guy from Minnesota thought he could tell a taller tale than a Texan and decided they would be the judges as to whether my story even ranked as a tall tale or just a little fib.

I told them it all started one day when it was real hot and humid and my brother and I wanted to go swimming to cool off. When we asked mom she said no because we were supposed to go with our folks to a wedding and we had to get dressed so there wasn't time for swimming. We didn't care much about going to the wedding but we got dressed up anyway. We were dressed before our folks were so we decided to go outside for awhile. We were kind of careful not to get our clothes dirty as we wondered around the farm. We found an old stock tank dad used to water the young stock and set it upright just for something to do. Then we remembered a bunch of dry ice dad had stored in an old trailer. We decided that if we melted the dry ice in the tank we could swim in it without getting our clothes wet because it was dry. So we got a bunch of it and put it in the tank, melted it and were swimming around in it until our mom yelled that it was time to go. We ran to the car got in and went to the wedding. Nobody suspected anything because we were dry and clean, and we forgot all about the tank full of melted dry ice until the next morning. It was late when we got home and we went right to bed. The next morning dad came busting into our room yelling about a couple dead calves. He demanded to know what we had done with that old stock tank. We both looked at each other knowing that we were busted and that it wouldn't do any good to try to shift the blame on someone else, because there wasn't anyone else to blame. We told him how we melted the dry ice in the tank and went swimming to cool off while we were waiting to go to the wedding. He told us to get dressed and get downstairs. When we got to the kitchen mom and dad were both there and mom gave us one of those looks that said we were in more trouble than even she could get us out of. Dad told us to follow him and walked out the door, and knowing that we had no choice we followed. When we got to the tank we realized that we had put it next to the corral where the steers were kept and that two of them had reached through the fence and drank the dry ice water. They were lying on the ground completely dehydrated because the dry ice water had dried them out. Dad gave us a lecture about how much money he would lose with the death of those two steers, and how he was going to take it out of our allowance until it was paid back to teach us to be more responsible.

When dad left we looked at each other and said how cool it was the way they had completely dried up just from drinking the dry ice water. Then we talked about how long it would take to pay for the cattle with our small allowance and tried to think of some way to get some money out of this situation. We decided that the hides would probably be worth a little money so we got some knives and started skinning them. Because the dry ice water had dried them so fast the meat hadn't had time to spoil and when we cut off a couple strips and dared each other to eat it we discovered that it wasn't too bad, just needed a little seasoning. We went into the kitchen and no one was there, so we searched through the cupboards and took a bunch of spices out to where we had cut up a bunch of the meat. We tried a lot of different combinations of spices and finally got the meat to taste good.

We then cut a lot of the meat and rubbed them in the spice mix, wrapped them in aluminum foil and put them in bags. We worked a long time and used up all the spices we could find. We then had no more spices. We looked at all the bags and wondered how to go about getting money out of it. We decided that our neighbor would know where we could take it to sell it so we loaded it into the baskets on our bikes and headed down the road to talk to him. He was a business man that worked in town and we thought he would know about selling our spiced meat. When we got to his place he was just getting home from work. He asked us what we had in the bags on our bikes and so we told him the story from start to finish. We then asked him if he could help us sell our spiced meat and he asked to try some. After biting off a piece and chewing it for awhile he said he thought it was pretty good and that people might buy it. He said the stuff was really tough and that you really had to jerk on it to get a piece off, and he then asked us what we called it, saying that we had to have a name other than spiced meat. We thought about it for a while and decided that we would call it jerky, because he had said that a person really had to jerk on it to get a piece off.

He said that might be a real good name and that he just might be able to sell it for us. We left all of the jerky we had made with the neighbor and went home thinking our troubles were over and we would be able to pay dad back for the steers and not lose our allowance.

When we went back a couple days later to see how much money we had made the guy told us he had taken out a patent on it in his name and that he owned the rights to it and we couldn't make or sell it without paying him a commission. He said because we had left all of the meat with him and hadn't told anyone else about making it we couldn't prove that it was our idea and we weren't going to get a single penny out of our invention. We didn't know what else to do so we just got on our bikes and went home.

And that's the true story of how my brother and I invented jerky and how the idea was stolen from us."

Max sat at the table and just looked across at Willie who was grinning like that school boy again. He finally said, "Willie that is the biggest bunch of crap I have ever heard in one story."

Willie just laughed and said, "I know, that's what those Texans said too, and it hurt them to admit that a Minnesotan had told it. They grudgingly admitted that I had told a tale that even they would have a hard time topping and to acknowledge defeat they made up that certificate."

They laughed together and Max said, "You always did have a weird imagination but I really think you've been alone in that truck to long."

Willie looked at Max with a hurt look in his eyes then the smile started from the corners of his mouth and he said," You know, that's exactly what I told Jean, and we decided that it was time for me to retire and the two of us spend some time together before it is too late to enjoy it. We decided that this was going to be my last trip and when we get back to Minnesota, after the reunion, I'm actually going to trade this old truck in on a new rig." Willie then reached into his shirt pocket and took out a folded piece of paper and handed it to Max. "This is going to be my next adventure," He said.

Max took the paper and unfolded it to reveal an advertisement for a mobile home. Max looked at the add and then looked at Willie, then back at the add. "You are serious aren't you?" he said as he looked back at Willie.

"You bet I am; I have been pounding across the country in this old truck and several others before it for too many years. We decided that it was time to let the younger generation have a chance at making a life for themselves and step aside. That's why I decided to ask you along on this trip. I figured it would be the last time I would be in California and I wanted to take at least one trip with you before I quit. Jean and I are going to travel around for a while and see all the things I've only been able to see on the road signs because trucks are not allowed on most of the tourist roads."

Max looked at the ad for the recreational vehicle and then back at Willie. He was thinking that He and Willie were about the same age, but that he had not given much thought to retirement. He and Sue had put money away and invested in a few stocks but had never really taken the time to discuss retirement. This revelation from Willie was a kind of eye opener and he didn't know quite how to process it.

"Sounds like you two have thought about this quite a lot. I guess Sue and I have been too busy trying to keep up our social standing and not let the younger generation better us that we haven't taken time to figure out just what it is that we are working for." Max handed the ad back to Willie and leaned back in his chair. This was a totally new aspect in his life and his analytical mind was busy processing it.

"Yes, Jean and I have talked about this quite a lot, but sometimes things are forced on a person without any way to change them." Willie quietly put the ad back into his shirt pocket and didn't say anything else.

Willie didn't say anything more and Max didn't ask, but as they finished their breakfast and after paying the bill; gathered up their things to head for the truck Max caught that look in Willie's eyes that suggested something had been lost. The feeling was quickly lost when they left the table and headed for the truck to start another day in this crazy adventure.

When they walked out of the building the sun was shining and it looked like it was going to be a nice day. They had to thread their way between trucks to get to where Willie had parked his in the second row. When Max cleared the back of the trailer he was walking past, and looked across the drive lane to find Willie's truck he missed it on the first sweep of the row. Then he looked again at the spot he thought the truck was parked in. He hadn't looked out the window this morning and now he couldn't believe what he was looking at. The dull and dirty truck they had arrived in last night had been transformed into a shining piece of chrome, paint and glass. He stared at the truck and then looked at Willie; standing beside him and smiling that impish smile he got when he had pulled off a successful prank or surprise.

"How do you like her now?" he beamed. "I hired a guy to clean it up a little. I had to take it to the truck wash on the other end of the parking lot, but he did the polishing while I was sleeping. He did a pretty good job, don't you think?"

"Wow, that guy must have worked all night to get it to look like this." Was all Max could say.

"Yea, he worked a long time on it. Did it real quiet, I slept right through it. He hasn't had much work for a while and he was glad to finally get some money."

Well, Max thought that explains the mystery man he had seen Willie talking to the night before. He had gotten up this morning and went straight to the shower and then busied himself packing and talking to Sue for a long time. It had been dark when he woke up and the curtains were closed, but if he would have looked out the window even in the dim light of the parking lot he would have seen Willie's truck shining like a beacon in the second row; looking like the day it was new.

Max walked around to the passenger side of the truck and took out the key Willie had given him to unlock the side compartment, and looking at the truck shining like new and the bright sun shining down on him, he almost forgot about the day he had had yesterday. As he opened the door to the side box a sudden noise a few trucks down brought all the images rushing back and he again wondered what Willies real motive for this trip was. He again thought about the bearded man in the restaurant handing Willie an envelope, about the crates of unknown contents in the trailer, the weigh station, which according to Willie, was never open, pulling them in and keeping them there for an hour. He thought about the two cars beside and in front of them that slowed down for no apparent reason then just sped away. As he put his bags in the side compartment he thought about rattlesnakes and wondered what strange things they would encounter today. He had been close to telling Willie that he didn't think the trip was going to work out. They were still close enough to California that he could have Sue drive to him and pick him up. He thought about telling Willie that if he still wanted him to go to the reunion he would drive to Minnesota with Sue and meet him there. It all made sense to him but when he had mentioned it to Sue she had argued that he hadn't really given the trip a fair chance and that they only had one full day and part of another one left before they got to Minnesota. As usual he had agreed with her and didn't say anything to Willie. He told her he would quit worrying about some conspiracy and enjoy the rest of the trip.

Max decided that Willie had really forgotten about the skunk incident and that he was actually trying to renew their old friendship in his own way. All of the thoughts about not continuing the trip happened last night in the hotel room and so had the decision to continue riding with Willie to the reunion. He tried to be positive and not worry but now that he was actually getting into the truck the doubts started again. The first one was a question he asked himself every time he called Sue. There was a click on the phone just before she answered and he couldn't figure out what it was. He imagined people in a crowded van with wire tapping equipment recording his calls and tracking them across the country. When he got into the truck and closed the door he felt a little more relaxed but he still had the feeling that they were being watched and Willie acted different from the way Max remembered him. Well, he thought, it was a long time ago and people do change, but he couldn't get over the feeling Willie was hiding something from him. He decided that there was no sense in being paranoid after all if he got in trouble he knew a good lawyer to call. As they started moving he settled into his seat, put on his sunglasses and prepared himself for whatever the day brought.

Chapter 3

They were out of control. The two girls had finished loading Sue's bags into the pickup, and with a wave to the security guard at the gate of what Sue called the high income upscale prison, they had left the gated community Sue lived in, and began an adventure four decades in the making. All of the "we should get together sometimes" had finally happened. They were free of all of the accumulated stress of their lives and were on one of the best adventures of their lives. It took Sue a couple miles before she could finally let herself relax and realize that she didn't have to worry about offending some rule of social grace. She was with Jean, the one person she could always be herself with.

Jean was used to the freedom of the road, having ridden with Willie on several trips, but still this was different. She was with a friend that she hadn't seen in years but still considered her best friend. They were together, driving across the country in an old pickup truck from so many years ago when life was still young and far less complicated. Willie had spent a lot of time looking for, and buying tapes of the bands they had listened to when they were young and worry free. He kept one set in the pickup and another identical set in the semi, and the girls were definitely enjoying the set in the pickup. They had driven through the chaotic traffic listening to Steppin Wolf and Aerosmith, Singing along with Credence and rocking to Led Zeppelin.

Now they were out of the California chaos and traveling through the beauty of the Rocky Mountains.

They had laughed, sang and talked until they were talked out and sore from laughing, but now Jean had gotten very quiet and Sue was wondering what was troubling her.

After long miles of silence she finally asked Jean what was bothering her.

Jean looked at her with a look that made Sue want to hug her, or hold her hand, or do something to comfort her. The hurt in her eyes was so unexpected and so deep but also so out of place in what had been such a fun filled trip that it took Sue completely off guard.

"Sue," she said "there's something about Willie I have to tell you". With those words Jean began a story that ended the lighthearted feelings of the trip for both of them.

When Jean had finished talking Sue sat in silence, staring out the windshield of the truck and not really seeing anything. She glanced out the side window, fidgeted with an imaginary piece of lint on her blue jeans but could not find any words to say.

"I don't mean to sound selfish or anything," she finally said after clearing her throat, "but is Max going to be safe riding with him?"

"Oh, yes, Willie knows all the back road short cuts and he'll get them to Minnesota," Jeans mood lightened a little when she talked about Willie and then she looked at Sue with a pleading expression in her eyes; "Please don't repeat any of what I told you to Max when he calls. It's better that he doesn't know."

For the next several miles Jean explained the details of Willies plan. Sue listened and when Jean finished talking she said "He's really gotten devious in his old age, hasn't he?"

They looked at each other and laughed, not the uncontrolled laughter of freedom like the beginning of the trip, but the laughter of two people who share a secret.

After a few miles of silence Sue looked at Jean and asked "well as long as we're involved in this crazy scheme of Willies we might as well enjoy ourselves. Do you trust us enough to get a room in a hotel with a bar?"

Jean looked at her friend and said "hell, ya" and the laughter and the music were back.

They drove along listening to music and talking but Jeans story about Willie had taken a lot of the lightheartedness out of the ride. There were long gaps in the conversation and some of the tapes would repeat a couple times before one of them would notice and change it.

When they finally decided to call it enough for the day it was getting late. They found a motel with a bar and restaurant and checked into a room. After getting luggage into the room and setting for a couple minutes Jean said there was one more thing they had to do before they could head to the bar and kick up their heels

They left the hotel and drove back the way they had just come from. It was dark when Jean began to slow down and put her signal on to make a left turn. The place they were entering was very puzzling to Sue and when Jean did not offer an explanation Sue began to wonder if she knew for sure what she was doing. Finally she asked Jean about it. "I know this has to do with Willie, but are you sure this is the right place? It doesn't even look like there is anyone here."

"I guess so," Jean answered not sounding totally convinced herself. As they exited the highway and drove down the road there were street lights that came on as they went under them and turned off again as they went by them, the next one would turn on as they approached it; lighting the way in to a large parking lot. They parked beside a large building and turned off the ignition and the lights plunging them in total darkness except for the distant lights on the highway. Sue quietly pushed the lock on her door and moved a little closer to the middle of the seat. Jean noticed her uneasiness and said "Willie is involved with a lot of different people and he said we could trust these guys so I guess we trust them. If only someone would show up to trust."

They had been sitting in the pickup for what seemed like hours, but was probably only about five or ten minutes when another vehicle entered the parking lot. The vehicle drove slowly down the road leading off the highway and the lights came on and went off showing its progress.

The vehicle made a wide turn around the lot and stopped a few feet from them facing directly at their windshield. "Nice touch," Sue whispered, "they could at least turn off their lights." As if on cue the lights went out and by the glow of the distant highway lights they watched as a very large person emerged from the vehicle and began walking towards them. "Trust Willie, he said it would be alright," Jean whispered; half for her benefit and half for Sue's.

The girls were very tired when they arrived back at the hotel, but they were determined to check out the bar and have a couple drinks and a dinner before going to bed.

They went to their room and washed off the road dust and with it some of the tension of the day disappeared so that by the time they strolled into the bar they were chatting and giggling and ready for a drink.

They picked a table next to the wall and settled in. There were not very many people in the room and the ones that were there were all paired up into couples. The place was quiet the talked in whispers so they wouldn't be heard, as if they had secrets to share with each other. They ordered drinks and a menu when the waitress came over to their table. The first drinks were gone quite fast and when they ordered the next round they decided they better order their meals also. This turned out to be a good decision because when the effects of the first drink were felt the reaction was not to get up and dance on the tables like a couple college age kids; it was two past middle age women who just wanted to eat their meal and get some sleep.

"See, I told you we could trust ourselves to behave in a bar without our husbands," Jean said through a very deep and long yawn as she slumped back in her chair and laughed; a very tired laugh.

"We better go before we fall asleep right here in our chairs," Sue said. They paid for the meals and drinks left a tip on the table and slowly walked back to their room. The end of a very strange and different day for both of them.

After yesterday Max was happy to have boredom set in. The ride was free the music was good and the scenery was beautiful. He asked Willie about the time he had spent in the Army and in Viet Nam, but Willie had said it was a long time ago, in a different world, and a different time. He said he didn't think about it much anymore and really didn't want to talk about it. He said he had done what he was told to do; was lucky enough to have gotten through it in one piece and come home, get married and spent his life enjoying what he had went there to protect. Max glanced at Willie as he drove the truck through the traffic; which on this stretch of road consisted of an occasional vacation vehicle and a few farm vehicles. He sat relaxed in the seat but there was a certain vigilance about him that Max couldn't quite understand. They had left the interstate highway and were traveling on a four lane road that wasn't as fast paced and busy as the "big road", as Willie called the interstate highway. The pace was more relaxed but Willie wasn't. As the day wore on he talked less and seemed to be looking for something and couldn't find it. They talked but the conversation always ended with Willie trailing off into himself and concentrating on driving and the occasional traffic. At times he would become alert and sit up straighter in the seat and become more focused on the traffic. At these times Max noticed a vehicle slowing down in front of them and through the round spot mirror on the driver's side front fender he could see a car in the lane beside the trailer not passing but just pacing them. The two vehicles would them slow down a little and force Willie to slow down with them. Willie would make some comment about stupid four wheelers, but Max became worried. When it happened Max could see no reason why they were doing it and he would wonder if maybe it had something to do with the crates in the trailer. What could these people want and why were they interfering with a truck on the highway. He wondered if they were just interfering with their truck or if they just liked to bother truckers. That didn't make any sense to Max and he decided it had to be connected to the mysterious crates in their trailer. He began to imagine that they were checking out there progress, waiting for the right time to stop them completely, not just slow them down. Maybe Willie was in some kind of partnership with them and this was some kind of a signal. Max realized he was being paranoid and that they were probably just what Willie said they were, stupid four wheelers.

At noon they stopped for lunch and sat talking and relaxing after they finished eating. Willie was more relaxed and even apologized for not being a better conversationalist while they were driving. He said all the years of driving along had become like a part of him and he wasn't used to having to speak his thoughts out loud. He said it was very different having another person in the truck with him. He told Max that if it made him feel any better the same thing happened when Jean would ride with him. He said that once he got into the truck and started driving he would zone out the rest of the world. It was his way of dealing with the constant need to concentrate on what was happening around him. He said he was aware of everything and involved with nothing.

If he saw an accident on the other side of the road he was aware of it but his attention was always on the traffic on his side of the highway. The traffic backup on his side of the road was always caused by people who slowed down to look at the accident and didn't watch the vehicle in front of them that was slowing down and they usually caused more accidents in the process. He said he couldn't understand people's fascination with death and injury. He said he had seen both of them close up and personal and that they were not pretty. That was as close as he came to talking with Max about Viet Nam.

After what turned out to be nearly an hour of talking Willie excused himself to go use the bathroom. He was gone for quite a while and Max was starting to become concerned, wondering if there was another bearded stranger meeting with him in the restroom. He was about ready to get up and go look for him when Willie rounded the corner and headed for the table. Max noticed a change in Willies step but dismissed it as the effects of a positive bathroom break.

Willie didn't return to his chair but stood by the table fishing money out of his billfold to leave as a tip. "I've already paid for the meal and left a tip", Max said, "It's the least I can do for getting a free ride to Minnesota."

Back in the truck and heading east there were gaps in the conversation as both of them got lost in their own thoughts. They were climbing in and out of some small mountains or large hills, depending on who was describing them. Max had been watching a small stream that would at times run alongside the road then disappear into a valley only to reappear after a few miles. "I wonder if there are any trout in that creek?" he said; more to himself than to anyone else.

"You know I've asked myself that very question every time I drive through this area," Willie said. Max jumped a little at the sound of Willie's voice. He hadn't realized he had actually voiced the question out loud. Willie went on to say that he had told himself that some day he was going to stop and check the stream out, but never had because he was always trying to make his delivery appointment. "I think this is someday," he said.

They drove in silence for a while and then Max noticed that they were slowing down. He turned his head away from the side window where he had again been watching the stream. He looked out the windshield expecting to see a vehicle slowing down in front of them, but the road was deserted. A glance in the spot mirror on the driver's side of the truck showed there was no vehicle there either. Puzzled he glanced at Willie. Willie had a sly smile on his face as he turned to look at Max. The smile was the same smile he got when he used to talk to people about where they had been fishing. It was a smile that said "I'm not telling you everything because it's a secret, and if I tell you it won't be a secret anymore."

His glance at Max ended when he turned back to look out the windshield and raised his arm to point to a wide spot on the shoulder of the road. This wide spot was what Willie was slowing down and aiming the truck at.

"I've looked at this spot every time I drive this road," he said. "I have never seen any trucks parked here but I keep thinking that trucks are what made it. The parking area on the shoulder allowed him to get the truck completely off the roadway and when he set the brakes he turned to Max and said," Yup, I think it's someday and this is the trip I've been waiting for. Let's go see if there are any fish in that creek.

Max was a little surprised but also excited. He had been watching the different streams as they appeared alongside the road then disappeared again and wondered if they were the same one or different streams flowing into a bigger stream then flowing into the oceans which connected all the streams flowing into them. Those thoughts were for a different time, now his thoughts were concentrated on the stream near the road.

"You bet I want to stop. Too bad we don't have any poles and a license for this state, I wonder if there are any worms around here, do you think the fish in these streams eat worms, do you know what kind of trout they have in the mountains?" It was only because he ran out of breath that he quit talking.

As Max threw open his door and jumped out of the truck Willie laughed to himself thinking it was a good thing Max had waited for him to stop the truck before he jumped out. Then he threw open his door and joined him on the bank of the stream. They were both as excited as when they were kids and were checking out a new fishing spot. They both stood on the bank of the stream watching the water swirl around rocks and listening to the sounds around them. They each followed the course of the water with their eyes, one following it up stream wondering where it came from and the other following it down stream wondering where it went to. After a long silence they both returned their gazes to the water in front of them.

The sun was midway down its slide towards the western horizon; the summer air was warm and smelled of wildflowers and mountain peaks covered with snow. There were many flying insects buzzing around the plants on the stream bank and many more hidden in the grasses. They all seemed to be singing at the same time. Many birds flew around them chasing the insects. Many more flitted about in the trees and bushes growing along the stream banks. After their scramble out of the truck and their dash down from the road to the stream, it was like they were put into freeze frame mode. They both just stood there moving nothing but their heads.

After the spell was broken by a splash upstream Willie turned to Max and said, "This is beautiful; I wish I had not wasted all of those trips through here and would have stopped just for a couple minutes to smell the air and hear the singing. It's amazing that this is just outside a quarter inch thick piece of glass and I never stopped to enjoy it."

Max was equally impressed. "You know, I have blocked all of this out of my life all the while I have lived in California. There are places just as nice as this not very far from where I live and I have never visited them, not once. It's sad, but I've been so caught up in chasing the almighty dollar and appearing socially correct that I have completely forgotten this feeling.

I haven't went that far," Willie said "I still fished and camped with Jean and the kids but since the kids have grown up and started lives of their own I've concentrated more on working. Trying to get that retirement fantasy so we can enjoy our so called golden years. At this moment it sure seems like a waste of a life. I could have enjoyed this moment every time I drove through here if I would have just pulled on to that wide spot on the shoulder. I've looked at it every time I've passed through here and every time I've said maybe next time I won't be in such a rush and will have more time, and then I can stop for a little while."

They both reached down and picked up a hand full of small pebbles from the sandy spot they were standing at and began tossing them into the stream. They used to do this when they were kids checking out a new fishing spot. They would try to scare the fish into leaving their hiding spot and if they found that there were a lot of fish they would return a couple days later with poles and bait. Today they didn't have long to wait to find fish. Their pebbles moved fish from undercuts in the bank where the grass hung down almost to the water, from the downstream side of rocks where the swirling water protected them from being seem from above and the rock protected them from the force of the current. For the next two hours they enjoyed themselves along and sometimes in the cold mountain stream. Anyone watching would probably have wondered what those two grey haired men were doing; but to the two guys running along the creek bank they were fifteen again and the only concern was not being late for chores and supper.

As the sun neared the horizon and a slight chill came with the breeze it also brought back reality and they realized they were quite a ways from the truck and that they were wet and dirty from the knees down. They also realized they didn't care; it had been the most enjoyable time either of them had had since that time so many years ago when their paths in life had separated. As they climbed up the steep bank to get onto the roadway and turned towards the truck they walked side by side with the fading sun on their backs and a smile on their faces; once again on the same path.

As they walked they didn't talk, they didn't have to, there were other ways for friends to communicate. When they reached the back of the trailer they separated and went up different sides. At the space between the cab of the truck and the trailer Willie told Max they had better get some dry clothes on, and there on the side of road in the middle of the mountains they both changed clothes and also values. They both began thinking about what kind of fishing poles they were going to buy.

Back in the truck they both sat relaxed in their seats. Willie started the diesel engine and sat looking out the windshield as the familiar vibration it sent through the whole truck steadily massaged him into the right frame of mind to continue the trip. They both would have been content to just sit there but the darkening of evening told them they had to go.

"I've always said that a person can't go back in time, when it's gone it's gone forever, but then I've always tried to make up time," Willie said making the quotation mark sign with his fingers as he said the last part. "Well, we are two hours later than if we wouldn't have stopped and we will just get to our stop for the night two hours later than if we hadn't stopped. I don't know about you but I think that two hours was worth every penny we didn't have to spend for them."

Max had his seat reclined back and just turned his head towards Willie, a smile on his lips and a sparkle in his eyes and all he said was "yea, I've got to get to a sporting goods store. I think I've had a relapse and an old addiction has returned."

Willie drove a little slower and seemed to Max to be a little less uptight. When they reached the truck stop Willie had picked out to stop at for the night, it was late and neither of them felt very hungry, so Max just grabbed his bag out of the side compartment and headed for the motel, as he did the night before. Willie stayed in the truck, again saying he couldn't sleep if he didn't know his truck was safe. Max found his room on the ground floor of the motel and let himself in. The curtain was open and as he pulled it closed he noticed his room faced away from the parking lot and towards the mountains they had just crossed. The peaks were bathed in moonlight and for a moment he stood and looked at them; a smile on his face, then he closed the curtains and dressed for bed; tonight no worries, and tomorrow Minnesota.

Max opened his eyes and looked at the darkness. Gradually his sight adjusted to the faint light coming in around the edges of the curtains. He hadn't just woke up; but had been lying in the bed with his eyes closed, but awake for some time. His thoughts had covered a wide range of subjects as they usually did when he let his mind escape the discipline of work and his daily routine. Mostly they floated around fishing poles and yesterdays stop in the mountains. The time the two of them had spent at that mountain stream had been one of the most relaxing times he had had for a very long time. His legs reminded him of how little he actually walked anymore, but the aches and pains were the good kinds that remind someone of a good experience.

His thoughts floated through his mind without control and eventually gravitated to the place they always arrive at. The event he wished he could surgically remove from his memory. As he lay in the bed reliving the scene of so many years ago he decided that today, before they reached Minnesota he was going to confront Willie and find out if he was still thinking about the incident, and if he held some kind of a grudge that had kept him from contacting him; or if it was really just the duties of life and family that had kept him away.

He thought back to the day he had pulled his car up and parked behind Willie's truck at the flower shop. The plan had been for him to go into the shop and distract Willie while his football buddies hid the package behind the seat of Willie's truck. Max went along with the scheme just to impress his peers on the team. After Willies accident and the forced separation due to the court proceedings they had drifted apart and Max had formed friendships with the guys he played ball with, and the two old friemds spent less time together; although they still got together for the occasional fishing trip or just to hang out at the drive-in; after the flower shop affair they would each go their separate ways for the next forty years.

The alarm on his clock went off just as he was remembering his part in the "stupidest thing he ever did", as he always referred to the prank that backfired.

He put those thoughts aside as he busied himself getting ready for the day and the last part of the trip. Their decision not to eat when they got to the truck stop, but to just go to bed was making itself known with a large rumbling in his empty stomach. He showered, dressed, packed and was heading to the truck in less than an hour. He made quite a bit of noise putting his bag into the side compartment of the truck, thinking Willie was still asleep and trying to wake him up so they could go get some breakfast, but there was no sign of life from inside the cab. Using the key Willie had given him he unlocked the passenger door of the truck, opened it and shouted up into the truck. After shouting twice and getting no response he climbed up in the seat and turning around he pulled the curtain to the sleeper area aside, but the bunk was empty. He decided that Willie must have been as hungry as he was and had gotten up early and went to the restaurant, and was there waiting for him now.

Max climbed down out of the truck closed and locked the door and turned to go to the restaurant. Instinct caused him to look to his left when he was about to cross the parking lot street and as he did so he caught sight of a figure standing by the front fender of a truck parked a little down the line from where he was. Although the sun was coming up it was still quite dark in the lot and the overhead lights were still on casting shadows on the ground. By their light Max was able to make out that the figure was Willie. Max stopped, hidden from sight by the truck next to him and the shadows from the overhead lights. He watched and could see that Willie was talking to someone, but that person was hidden by the trucks and Max couldn't see who it was. Willie was talking to the other person, but he kept glancing towards his truck as if waiting for someone. Max watched for awhile then hunger got the best of him and he decided to go to the restaurant and wait for Willie. He thought about going to see who Willie was talking to but decided it was not his business. All the years of driving the same route Willie probably knew half the drivers here. What's so strange about him talking to one while he waited for his passenger to get up? Max reasoned with himself, and fought valiantly against the paranoid fears of the first day of the trip. He tried hard to bring back the feelings of the day before at the mountain stream. He had almost succeeded as he started across the street when he glanced in Willies direction. Out in the open he was in plain sight of Willie and whomever he was talking to. Willie glanced his way at the same time Max started walking and waved when he recognized him.

Max still could not see who it was that Willie was talking to but after the wave he turned back to the person and extended his hand towards them. Max saw the head of the other person lean towards Willie and he realized it was a female. Willie leaned forward and gave her a quick kiss and then turned and headed towards him.

Max decided not to say anything to Willie about what he had seen, after all he hadn't been in contact with Willie since that day so many years ago, and had no idea how his life had evolved and how his private life at home was. He knew he was still married to Jean and that he had seemed happy in his marriage when he had talked about it, but Max had no way of knowing how stable their relationship was. If Willie had other women in his life that was none of his business and he wouldn't make any judgments about it. By then Willie had caught up with him and Max couldn't think of how to start a conversation so he just said, "friend of yours," indicating the person Willie had been talking to.

"You might call her that," Willie said, looking back at the spot where the other person had been. That was all that was said about it and they both turned their attention to their growling stomachs.

There was not much conversation as they ate. They were both hungry and concentrated on filling the void in their midsection left by their decision not to eat the night before.

After a few minutes of eating in silence Willie asked "have you ever heard how much an out of state fishing license costs?"

Max stopped eating for a moment and thought, trying to remember if he had ever heard of someone in California buying an out of state license. He finally decided that he hadn't and that each state was probably different and that it probably depended on whether it was a seasonal or temporary license. Then they began discussing the different poles and bait and the effect of hatching insects on the ability of an angler to catch fish. They were still talking about fishing when they went through the automatic procedure of paying for the meal, going to the bathroom, walking to the truck and climbing into their seats. They were still talking about fishing when Willie started the engine and they began the last part of their trip.

They were still talking about fishing as Willie pulled out of the parking lot, onto the highway and pointed the big truck northeast and they headed towards Minnesota.

They merged into the light traffic and were soon out of what Willie called the secretary five hundred. The morning race when everyone was going to work. He said it was always nice to be heading out of town in the morning because the traffic was all on the other side of the highway making it easier to get going and not have to fight for a piece of the highway.

The drive home began with the two of them talking about fishing, past and future. They reminisced about fishing trips they had taken together always stopping short of talking about the accident or things that had happened after it. Max decided not to bring up any of those memories, especially not the one he wanted so very much to forget.

They talked about trying to find time in the few days Max was going to be in Minnesota to get in at least one short fishing adventure. Willie said the worm digging fork was still hanging in the garden shed where it always was.

When Willie mentioned the fork and the garden shed Max was struck with a sudden dose of reality; no matter how much they talked about the old times he realized they were gone; along with his boyhood home. When his parents had died the farm was sold and the new owners had completely removed, disassembled they had called it, every building on the place. In their place they had built a large house and a large horse barn, which they insisted on calling a stable. Neither Willie nor Max could see the logic in owning horses that were never ridden, but there were a lot of people who had horses as a kind of status symbol.

Willie seemed to sense where Max's thoughts were going because he told him not to worry, that he would let him use his fork seeing as how he didn't have one of his own. That got a smile out of Max and relived his melancholy mood.

As the miles rolled away the talk slowed and finally the silence of boredom set in. They had caught all the trophy trout in their imaginations, talked over all types of poles, agreed that natural bait was still the best, and now there was nothing left to discuss on the subject. They drove, not in silence but not talking, as Willie continued to play his cassette tapes as he had during all the lapses of conversation during the trip. He didn't play them loud, just loud enough. They both floated back in time, together in the truck but separate in their thoughts, and the miles rolled on. As the day wore on they got closer to the end of the trip and their mood and restlessness increased.

Willie talked about getting rid of his truck and trailer, trading them in on a new rig. When Willie talked about retirement Max could see that it wasn't what he really wanted; whenever he mentioned it he would get quiet for a while afterwards. Max figured it was just sentimentality over giving up a way of life he had spent so many years doing.

There was a lot of sadness in Willie's voice whenever he talked about getting rid of his truck, but Max noticed a hint of tiredness in his actions also. It was as if there was an acceptance of something he couldn't control.

As they crossed the border into Minnesota Willie looked at Max and asked if he felt any different being in his home state. "How long has it been since you were in Minnesota?" he asked Max.

Max thought for awhile and them said, "Boy, it's been quite awhile, probably fifteen years. Time sure slips away doesn't it?" he said.

Willie looked at Max then turned to look back through the windshield "Yes, it sure does," he said quietly.

After that there was another period of silence when they were both lost in their own thoughts, listening to the music and watching the countryside roll by. For Willie the scene was a familiar sight. He gauged the distance to their destination by the landmarks they passed. For Max it was a totally new experience. As they got closer to the end of the trip and to their childhood home Max began to recognize buildings and places from when they traveled these roads together. But he also recognized and commented on how much had changed.

Willie was surprised when Max mentioned things that used to be there and were now gone. He realized how routine the trip had become and how quickly a person accepts change and forgets the past.

When he began seeing road signs telling him the distance to their destination Max realized the trip was over and he wasn't in jail or laying dead in a road ditch after the truck had been robbed. He felt a little foolish about his fears and thoughts about international smugglers, and was glad he hadn't said anything to Willie about it.

Willies spirits picked up also. He talked about getting the freight unloaded and taking a couple days off before starting his next adventure.

"That R.V. is going to be a big change for you. No appointment deadlines to meet, no weigh stations to worry about; just pick up and go whenever and wherever you and Jean decide to." Max was talking but he could tell Willie was not listening. Probably just concentrating on getting the freight delivered, he thought to himself.

After another few miles of quiet Willie pointed at the clock on the dash and commented about the art of scheduling. "We have a three o'clock appointment, we are four hours from our delivery location and it's eleven o'clock. Not bad timing if I do say so myself. Even with the stop in the mountains we are still going to be on time."

Willie pulled into a rest area not far from the delivery site to use the bathroom and call the warehouse to confirm that he was going to be on time for his delivery. While he was talking to the person at the warehouse Max looked around the rest area and the neighboring fields to see if he could recognize anything familiar. Suddenly he was very interested in what Willie was saying. He didn't turn his head but he concentrated on what Willie was saying. Willie informed the person on the other end of the phone line that the two crates were still in the trailer and in good condition. He then informed that person to contact a third person to tell them to be at the warehouse on time to pick up the crates before someone else got them, or they got lost in the confusion of unloading. Suddenly Max found himself looking for rattlesnakes in the rest area.

Max's paranoid thoughts were set in motion again at the mentioning of the crates. He had actually put them out of his mind for most of the day as they had gotten closer to the end of the trip, and nothing had happened. When they got back into the truck to drive the last few miles of the trip Max found himself looking closely at the few trucks that shared the rest area parking lot with them. He didn't know what he expected to see but after only a couple days in the trucking world it was still a very strange and unknown place to him.

As they drove out of the lot and onto the drive leading to the highway Max studied the vehicles in the lot on the other side of the building, cars, pickups, a few campers, and SUVs'. He watched the people going about their business and he thought, "They all look normal to me, but then isn't that what they say about sociopaths; that they look just like everybody else? Max old boy, he thought you are really way too paranoid."

He turned to look at Willie and asked how long the unload process usually took once they got to the warehouse.

Willie said the place they were going to was the best place he had ever found to unload at. They weren't like most warehouses where the workers could care less about the driver and never talked or even acknowledged they were there. All they cared about was unloading the trailers and the driver was of no concern to them. They are protected by the union and paid by the hour; they don't care if they work or not they still get paid. The place they were going to unload at was very different. It was a small company and the dock workers were friendly and actually talked to the drivers as friends. They asked how the trip was and were actually interested. They worked together to get the freight unloaded and to get the trucker on their way to their next appointment. "Once we get to the dock and the paperwork comes through it usually takes about twenty minutes to unload a truck. Depending on the number of trucks ahead of us, and whether they are on schedule, and there are no breakdowns, we should be in and out of the place in less than two hours."

As they drove into the warehouse facility Max was looking at the size of the complex and at all the trucks coming and going and he thought that Willie's estimate of two hours was not going to happen. He looked at Willie and didn't see any signs of concern about the number of trucks so he relaxed a little and thought maybe this was the way it always was.

Willie glanced at Max at the same time and noticed his concern, "Coordinated chaos," was all he said and turned back to guiding the truck through it.

Willie drove like he was pulling into his driveway at home. Arm out the open window slowly but steadily weaving through the maze of trucks determined to get to the check-in door. Max questioned Willie about his idea of a small company as they made their way down the central roadway in this huge lot with large warehouses on both sides, and more visible in the distance. Willie explained that although they were in this huge complex there were many individual companies sharing the buildings, and that the place they were going was housed in one of the buildings on the other side of the lot in front of them.

After slowly making their way across the lot they came to a gate in the fence separating this part of the complex from the rest of it. Willie stopped beside a speaker on a post positioned at the height of a truck window. He pushed the talk button and announced his presence to the person on the other end. After a few moments a voice from the speaker asked for his delivery number and Willie rattled off a string of numbers from the freight bills he held in his hand. After another short wait the voice sounded again and said "Hello, Willie; back into your usual door." Then it went silent and the gate in front of them began sliding open.

The complex they were entering was a scaled down model of the rest of the large facility behind them. The lot was fairly large with three buildings, one on each side and one directly ahead of them. Willie noticed Max was looking a little lost and said, "The building to the right is dry goods, the building in front of us is frozen goods and the one to the left is perishable; which is where we are heading.

The line of trucks they had been following had disappeared, with some of them turning off at different places to go to other buildings until they had became the only truck going in this direction. It was then that Max understood Willies unconcern about the number of trucks in the yard when they arrived. As they approached the building Max read the sign over the front door giving the company name. He was amazed when he realized where he was. "How in the world did this place get so big?" he asked. "I remember when we were kids driving by this place to go fishing. It was just a small building with a few doors."

"Yea, this place was way out in the country when we used to go to that little creek to go fishing. Now that creek is a cement spillway through the back side of the complex we just drove through. The people who own this business owned a large chunk of land and they sold it to the corporation that put up the rest of this place. They kept their original business and have managed to stay in business despite the competition. Just try to imagine how many more people there are in the area now compared to when we were young. As I've watched it grow over the years I've wondered if it would ever stop, and I've come to the conclusion that it won't." Willies last comment had a note of either defeat or acceptance that Max found a little disturbing.

As they got closer to the warehouse and the door designated as Willies they passed the lot where the employees parked their vehicles. Max was absently looking at the vehicles when one of them caught his eye. It was a black four door sedan with the windows tinted so dark a person couldn't see into it. It looked completely out of place in a lot filled with older pickups with firewood, car parts and an assortment of other items in their boxes. There were jeeps with smiley faces covering their spare tires and sport utility vehicles with compact disks hanging from their rear view mirrors. But only one dark sedan with tinted windows.

As they got closer Max noticed that the driver's window was open about three inches, but when they got close it closed quickly. The window closed quickly, but not before Max caught a glimpse of the driver. Max was sure that the driver was the same person Willie had talked to in the truck stop restaurant the morning they left California. That doesn't make any sense Max thought. It was a man with a beard, that much he was sure of, but if the guy was coming to Minnesota anyway why did he have Willie bring the crates in the back of a trailer loaded with produce? Then he thought if the guy was really involved in something illegal he wouldn't take the chance of been pulled over with the contraband in his vehicle. This can't be good he thought.

Max looked at Willie then pushed his head deep into the seat back and looked straight ahead.

Willie maneuvered the truck and trailer through the lot and swung around to the back of the building, there he made a wide swing and began backing into door number one hundred and thirteen. After setting the brakes and gathering up the paperwork he put his hand on the door handle, looked at Max and said, "It's show time,"."

Willie had stopped and opened the trailer doors before he put the trailer completely up to the dock, so when Max got out of the truck he walked around the front of the cab to the driver's side and caught up with Willie who was already heading to the service entrance door. I hope he means it is just time to unload the trailer and that this doesn't turn into a nightmare ordeal involving police and customs agents and government officials from several different governments. Max looked around the lot as he hurried to catch up with Willie and realized they were the only truck on this side of the building.

The service door was numbered one hundred and ten so it was close to their dock." It's nice that they gave us a door close to the service entrance," Max commented as they opened it and entered. "Yea, they treat me pretty good here," Willie said. "I've been delivering here for a long time, and I've always gotten a door close to the walk-in door. Of course that was easy years ago because there weren't that many doors." They entered the warehouse and headed towards their dock. Max noticed the yellow squares next to each dock and felt proud that he knew what they were for.

Willie opened the dock door and set the ramp in place. After removing his load locks and standing them against the wall in the yellow square he stopped and looked up and down the length of the warehouse. The side they were on was deserted except for the two of them. The other side was a different story. There were trucks in several of the doors and they were being unloaded by a small army of forklifts that seemed to be completely out of control. To Max it looked like a sea of confusion, but Willie stated that every thing seemed to be going smoothly and they should be out of there in no time.

As Max looked around he couldn't believe they would be out of the warehouse in less than a half hour as Willie had said. There were so many trucks along the other side of the warehouse floor that it seemed to Max it would take all day to get them unloaded, but as he watched he began to see that what at first had looked like mass confusion was in fact a well played ballet. He noticed that each truck had three forklifts and three workers on the floor and they worked at a speed that was not a mad dash and scramble, as it had first appeared, but was instead, a coordinated sequence of events that moved the freight from the truck to the cooler very efficiently. One driver entered the trailer and reappeared with a pallet, while still backing up after he cleared the end of the trailer he sat the pallet on the floor and another lift driver would pick it up from the side and set it in the middle of the warehouse floor. There a team of workers would take layers off the pallet and stack them onto another pallet, making them the size needed to fit into the racking system in the cooler. After the pallets were made the right height they were tagged and shrink wrapped and a third lift driver appeared to move them to the cooler. This went on until the entire trailer was empty. Then the entire team moved to another trailer and the dance began again. Not all of the pallets needed to be broke down and these were tagged and moved away quickly.

Max was amazed at how steadily they worked and commented on the fact to Willie. Willie said that the warehouse only received freight for eight hours a day five days a week, and that after the big rush the workers got a break and then they began picking the different items that made up the delivery loads taken to the different companies the warehouse serviced. That process was a lot less rushed and they could work at a slower pace." It's a pretty cool operation. Slackers don't last very long here, and the best thing is that it isn't management that gets rid of them it's their fellow workers. They have a profit sharing plan and the more freight they move through here the more chance of a profit. Management is very fair and that's the key to their success. They are very open and honest with the financial reports and the employees can see how their efforts are rewarded. If someone doesn't want to keep up their share of the work they don't work here.

Just as the team across the floor from them finished with the truck they were unloading everything stopped. It was as if someone had pulled a plug somewhere and cut all power to everything and everyone. "Break time," Willie said, "That's the problem with getting a later unload time. I usually get the first slot in the morning so I'm out of here and home by nine o'clock. I didn't know how things would go on this trip so I asked for a later unload time. The good thing is that they are as efficient at break as they are at work." Max was amazed that fifteen minutes after everything had came to a standstill it started up again, as if the plug was reconnected and power restored.

The three o'clock time slot was for trucks that had trouble and needed a late appointment. There were only three trucks at the dock doors including theirs. When the unloading teams began to unload these trucks another team of workers appeared. They drove scaled down street sweepers and began cleaning up the trash left from the unloading of thousands of tons of freight. They worked from the far end of the building towards the end with the three trucks being unloaded.

"How does it feel to be delivering your last load of freight?" Max asked as he watched the forklift driver enter their trailer.

"I don't know how I feel, I've thought about this day for quite a while and now that it is happening it doesn't seem like its real." Willie was talking to Max but he was looking at the activity going on around them. He was watching the drivers with a very real look of sadness. He knew each of the drivers personally and they knew him. It was obvious that they knew it was his last load but there seemed to be a feeling of finality about it above just retiring from driving.

Some of the other team members were finished with the truck they were working on and came over to help unload Willie's. When the forklift driver was about to back out of the trailer with a pallet they would sound their horn to warn people who might be standing in the way. When all the crews were working it had been a non-stop chorus of horns, but now that there was only one trailer being emptied the lone horn echoing off the walls sounded sad and kind of lonely.

When the driver brought the last pallet off the trailer he gave a double blast of his horn to inform the rest of the crew that the load was finished. With the double blast Willie told Max he had to go talk to some people in the office about his paper work and that he would be right back. With that statement he was gone, walking away down the warehouse towards a door on the other side of the building. Max stood in the yellow square and didn't really know what to do. He decided to pick up the load locks and put them in the trailer for Willie and when he entered the trailer he looked up its length and suddenly stopped moving. There up against the front wall sat the two crates.

The driver of the forklift that had been unloading the trailer had disappeared down the warehouse floor but now he was coming back with an empty pallet and stopped at the rear of the trailer. Max slowly recovered his ability to move and stepped out of the trailer so the driver could get in, and as he did so he looked around the warehouse. What he had expected to see he didn't know, but what he saw almost made him run for the door.

The two women sat in the pickup slumped in their seats and not talking. For a long while they sat in silence then Sue turned her head towards Jean and said, "I wish it was mine."

"What are you talking about? You have a beautiful home," Jean exclaimed.

"Yes, it's very nice. Max and I have planned and built it together and made it just what we want; but I have never quite gotten used to California. I guess I'm getting older and have been thinking about Minnesota more lately. California was fun when we were younger and had the kids home, but it is a young person's state. I miss Minnesota and friends like you and Willie. We have friends out there but, oh, you know what I mean." Sue sat back and silently looked at Jeans house. Then they both decided that they should grab some bags and go inside before the neighbors started talking. Which got a laugh out of both of them because the nearest neighbor was a half mile down the road.

"What neighbors?" Sue had said when Jean had said it. "There is still a half mile between you and the next farm house. That's what I miss the most, space to sit in the yard and not have to impress the neighbors."

They both got out of the truck and went to the tailgate end. After pulling the latch and sliding the bed drawer out, as Jean called the storage compartment Willie had made for the pickup, They each picked up two bags and walked up the sidewalk to the house. Jean turned the knob and opened the door and Sue exclaimed, "You didn't even lock the door when you left!"

Jean laughed and said, "Don't be silly; this is not the fifties or sixties that we grew up in. We lock the door every time we leave, but I told the neighbors that were watching the place to leave it open today after they checked on everything because we were going to be home and they could leave the key on the kitchen table. I figured I would probably have a mess in my handbag and didn't want to have to empty it out trying to find the keys. I wish it was still like it was, but things have changed here just like out there."

"One thing is still the same," Sue said, "You still say kitchen instead of dining room." And they both had to set the bags down and laugh.

Jean stepped back after pushing the door open and indicated that she wanted Sue to go in first.

Sue turned a little sideways so the bags she was carrying would fit through the door and looking down so she didn't trip over the threshold, and stepped in to the living room of Jean and Willies old farm house country home. She turned herself back to face into the room; looked up and began to cry.

Jean had entered behind her and stood beside her also looking up, only she was smiling.

"I didn't mean to make you cry." She said to Sue as they stood looking at the large banner hung across the far wall of the room.

The banner read "My dearest friend, welcome to my home" and it had an enlarged picture of the two of them sitting on a car hood at the local drive-in; only they were quite a lot younger in the picture.

As they had done in Sues house that first day when Jean had entered they turned towards each other and hugged, a long time until it became awkward leaning over two bags on the floor between them, then they let go of each other and turned back and looked in silence at the banner.

"I still have that picture too, "Sue said.

"I know, I saw it in the frame on your mantle. I almost spoiled this when I saw it there. I came close to telling you about this, but I'm very proud of myself for not saying anything. You know how hard it is for me to keep a secret." She was holding Sues hand and gave it a little squeeze, "We sure messed up letting those two boys keep us apart all these years just because of their little hissy fit."

"We sure did," Sue said. And she squeezed back.

After standing just inside the open doorway and looking at the banner in silence for a long time; each of them rolling the film of their memories, of time spent together as kids, through the projector in their minds; they both arrived at the present at the same time and with a deep sigh of contentment. Jean said, "Grab the bags and I will show you where you and Max will be staying while you are here."

It took four trips each but they finally got all the luggage and other items from the trip unloaded and in the house. None of it was put away but it was all in the house, and Jean said that was good enough for a while.

Jean guided Sue to the glider swing on the back porch and they both collapsed into its cushioned comfort. They sat talking and swinging for a very long time, two friends who's paths had been separated by love and family long ago, and now had come together. They were at peace and life was good at the moment, and neither of them wanted it to end.

But like all good things it came to a sudden end when Jean realized what time it was, "Oh, my gosh, we have to go." And she grabbed Sues hand and they ran to the pickup. This time Jean really did leave the door unlocked when they left.

On the way through the house Jean had grabbed a set of keys off a hook by the front door and tossed them to Sue, telling her to take the jeep because she wasn't sure how things were going to turn out and her and Max might need some transportation of their own; besides she said, "There's only room for two in Willies pickup."

Sue backed the jeep out of the garage and Jean checked the back of the pickup, making sure she had closed and locked the end gate and that she had everything she needed for what she was about to do. She wished she could just sit and talk with Sue but she said there would be plenty of time for that later. She just hoped everything went according to Willie's plan. In a small part of her mind she felt sorry for Max but then she rationalized it by saying he actually deserved it. She noticed that Sue had pulled up and was ready to go so she gave her thumbs up and ran to the cab of the pickup and got in. She started the engine and they headed for the warehouse where Willie and Max were unloading the trailer.

When she pulled out onto the road she slipped one of Willies tapes into the player and the Doors started signing "Riders on the storm." That fit her mood perfectly because there was a very big storm brewing in her life. Checking to make sure Sue had made it out of the driveway and onto the road she began thinking about the changes that were going to take place in her life, and now that she was alone she began to cry.

Max watched as the small crowd of people, less than a half dozen, as far as he could make out from this distance; walked towards him down the long warehouse floor. They had entered the warehouse at the far end and the distance was too great for Max to make out any faces, although he was certain that one of them had a beard and the closer they got to him the more sure he was that that person was the guy from the restaurant in California. As they got closer he started to study the faces and he had the strange feeling that he knew a couple of them from somewhere. They were now about one hundred feet away and Max could tell for sure that the one with the beard was the guy Willie had called the professor.

At that moment there was a blast from a horn behind him and Max almost lost control. He jumped and turned at the same time and moved to the yellow square. He looked into the trailer and saw the lift driver backing towards the ramp and coming out with the two crates on the empty pallet he had taken in a few moments before. When he cleared the end of the ramp he lowered the pallet to the floor and as it contacted the floor and began to slip off the forks he kept backing, when the forks cleared he raised them a couple inches and sped away towards the cooler and was gone through the door in a flash. He sure seemed to be in a hurry to get out of here Max thought.

As he watched the lift driver disappear through the cooler door he caught sight of some movement to his left, opposite the direction of the approaching men. He turned and what he saw caused the color to leave his face, and he began to sweat despite the coolness of the warehouse.

He looked around quickly to see if Willie was anywhere in sight but he was still in the office getting his paperwork.

The two groups of men arrived at the same time to where Max was frozen to the floor inside the yellow square. They formed a half circle facing him and the two crates sitting on the pallet in front of him. As Max looked from face to face he got the disturbing feeling that he knew some of the men from the second group as well as the ones he thought he recognized from the first group. That is crazy he told himself. How could he possibly know any of these people? They were much younger than he was, and were obviously locals from the area and he hadn't been back here in years. He was sure that aside from the guy with the beard and long coat he had not seen any of them before.

"What's in the crates?" One of the men from the second group asked. There were six of them and they were all wearing police uniforms.

"I don't know. They are not mine. They belong to the guy who owns the trailer, and to that man," Max said and pointed to the bearded person standing to his right.

Max was getting a little angry and very nervous, "Where's Willie?" he thought." Why did he run off just when the crates were going to be unloaded?"

Max tried to remember what Willie had said about the guy with the beard. Something about the invasion of Iraq, and the looting of the museum in Bagdad. Could this be a conspiracy between Willie, the guy in the long coat, and these guys dressed in police uniforms, to ship stolen artifacts across the country and have him get the blame? "That's crazy," Max thought. "Willie couldn't be holding a grudge that strong, and for this long, over something that happened forty plus years ago; could he? Had he been scheming all these years about how and when to get even?" Max remembered how embarrassed he was in front of his girl friend, now wife, over the stupid prank he and his football buddies had played on him. It had been a very important time in Jeans life, her first prom, and in Willies life, his first real date.

He could still see Willie standing by his pickup truck holding the bag and yelling at the top of his voice, "I'll get even with you if it's the last thing I do."

Chapter 4

When Willie had entered the flower shop to buy the corsage for Jean Max had parked behind him, along with three members of the football team. They had convinced Max to go along with a plan to embarrass Willie; and Max, thinking that it would improve his standing in the good-ol-boys club, had performed his part; a part that caused him to regret his actions for four decades.

His part in the plan was to go into the shop and distract Willie while the others put a bag in his truck behind the seat. When he entered the flower shop the others had gotten out of the car and removed a paper bag from inside three layers of plastic bags. In the bag was a dead skunk. The idea was that because of Willies injury he wouldn't be able to smell the skunk and when he picked up Jean she would make such a scene because of the smell he would be so embarrassed that he would just go home and his date would be spoiled and they would have a big laugh at his expense. It was a stupid and childish plan and

Max could not understand why these guys did things like that to Willie, just because he couldn't smell. The only reason Max went along with it was because the captain of the football team; and self proclaimed leader of the god-ol-boys club had promised him that he could play in the homecoming game that night. Being late to join the team, Max didn't get a lot of play time and this was a chance to impress Sue.

When Max and Willie came out of the flower shop the other three were back in Max's car and they smiled and waved at Willie as he got in his truck and drove off to pick up Jean.

They laughed and buddy punched each other all the way to the school, where they went to get ready for the game.

They were curious when they saw Willies truck parked in front of the school when they arrived and looked at each other a little guiltily wondering if he had found the bag and was waiting for them.

There were quite a few other kids standing around and they noticed they were standing in groups as if they were waiting for something to happen. It turned out that someone smelled the skunk and that they had found out about the plan to embarrass Willie, and just wanted to see his reaction when Jean got into the pickup and smelled the skunk.

Willie had told Jean he would pick her up at the school where she was hanging out with Sue. Sue was a member of the cheerleading team and was going to practice before the game. Jean was nervous and just needed the moral support of her close friend before her big date.

Max parked his car a short distance from Willies truck on a side street where Willie wouldn't notice him, they didn't have long to wait before a stir began to spread through the groups of people standing around the school. When Jean and Willie came out of the building it was obvious that Jean had notice the smell because she kept looking at Willie and quietly covering her nose. The smell of the skunk was quite strong even at the distance Max was parked from the pickup and they knew Jean could smell it as she approached Willies truck but she got in and slid across the seat without saying anything. This was a disappointment to the guys with Max as they had expected her to react differently.

When Jean was seated on the passenger side of the truck she couldn't take the odor any longer. Two things happened at the same time; neither of which the good-ol-boys had anticipated. Jean hurriedly opened the passenger door and leaning out she threw up; and Willies sense of smell returned. The nerves which had been damaged in the accident chose that moment to begin sending signals to his brain. Doctors who examined him later offered no explanation as to why it happened at that moment other than to say that perhaps the overpowering strength of the odor from the cab of the truck, which had been closed while Willie was in getting Jean, was enough to kick start the nerves working again. But one thing was certain, the nerves were working; after one breath he too vomited. Jean left the truck as soon as she could manage to get her breathing and gagging under control and Willie, despite his urge to vomit searched the vehicle for the source of the smell. When he discovered the bag behind the seat he pulled it out and threw it into the street. Standing by his pickup and looking hurt and confused he noticed Max's car and the three passengers laughing uncontrollably with Max sitting behind the steering wheel looking very ashamed and afraid. Willie walked over to the bag and despite the smell he picked it up and extending it towards Max he shouted at the top of his voice that he would get even with him for this if it was the last thing he ever did.

He tossed the bag down in Max's direction, walked over to Jean and said something to her, closed the passenger door, walked around to the driver's side and got in. It was like a freeze frame moment with the only movement being Willie. None of the people standing around said anything or even moved as he closed the door and drove away. He drove down the street looking straight ahead with his hands clenching the steering wheel so tight the knuckles turned white. He drove slowly to the end of the street, stopped for the stop sign, turned the corner and was gone from sight before anyone moved.

For a few moments after he left every one stood in silence. Sue, who had been standing on the school steps, was the first to move. She ran down the steps to Jean who was still standing where Willie had talked to her. Despite the mess on hers dress Sue hugged her friend tight and then the two of them walked together to the school.

Sue turned to look at Max and the look on her face convinced him that no matter how many games he played in she was not going to be impressed with him for a very long time, and it would be a very long time, if ever, before she forgave him for his part in this stupid prank.

As they walked back to the building everyone there began moving at once. The three guys with Max began laughing and buddy punching each other again, they got out of the car and started belly bumping each other like they had just scored a winning point in an important game. Max watched them and realized how stupid he had been to go along with them in their prank, and how his thoughts of impressing Sue had totally backfired and that he had probably lost her and his one true friend.

When the three guys finally settled down he told them that he quit the team and wouldn't be playing in the homecoming game that night. He then got into his car and drove off in the opposite direction that Willie had taken.

After a few moments of mixed reactions to what had just happened everyone went about their business and the one thing on everyone's mind was homecoming.

A few moments later everyone in the vicinity of the school building stopped what they were doing and stared down the street in the direction from which Willie had driven away. Slowly coming up the street was an ugly yellow green or green yellow pickup. No one had expected to see Willies truck so soon after what had happened. On other occasions when he had been pranked Willie had just disappeared for a couple days, but today was different.

Up the street from the same direction he had left, Willie drove his truck. His hands gripping the wheel in the same death grip of determination as when he had left. Looking straight ahead he drove to the curb opposite the spot he had been parked in earlier. He got out and walking around to the passenger side of the vehicle he removed a large box, and with that tucked under his arm he walked to the school. He continued looking straight ahead and gave no acknowledgement to the people he passed on his way. He entered the building and when he had disappeared through the doors there was a sudden rush of people running to the doors, curious to see what he was up to.

He walked straight down the hallway not moving for anyone he met. He looked straight ahead and the kids that he passed noticed that there were tears on his cheeks.

He went directly to the girl's locker room and knocked on the door. He waited and when the door opened it was Jean who opened it. They stood looking at each other for a while and then he handed her the box. The only words spoken were when Willie said, "We'll skip dinner and I will pick you up at seven to go to the prom. Please put this dress on. I hope it fits."

Jean wiped her eyes with her hands and reached out to take the box from Willie. Wiping her eyes had smeared her makeup and with the front of her dress soiled she looked like anything but a girl waiting for her first prom. Willie had driven to the dress shop and bought the first formal gown he saw that he thought was close to her size. Like the rest of the girls going to the prom Jean had spent a lot of time and money on her dress, choosing just the right one then having it altered and sized to look just right, and in the few moments outside the school all of that had been ruined. All Willie had told her when he had left was that he would be back and she had been crying with Sue because she thought her evening had been totally ruined. She could not believe that her prince charming was standing in front of her, still asking her to be his date for the evening.

When she reached out and took the box all he said was, "Seven o'clock at Sue's house," and he left.

"Where is the driver?" The question brought Max out of his stroll down memory lane and back to reality.

"I don't know. He said he had to get his paperwork signed and went through that door." Max indicated a door with an exit sign over it across the warehouse floor.

"I don't know how he is going to get his paperwork signed out there. That door leads to the employee parking lot." The officer then began looking at Max and asked the person in the long black overcoat if he recognized him.

The guy looked at Max and said he was definitely the one who had remained at the table while the other one talked to him about shipping the crates to Minnesota.

The policeman turned to Max and said, "Well, if these aren't your crates you shouldn't have any objections if we open them and see just what is in them."

"No objections what so ever." Max replied.

Then the policeman sent someone to get a pry bar to open the crates, and while they waited Max began to look around at the ten men facing him over the two crates resting quietly on the pallet between them. Five of the men had uniforms and were wearing guns. The other four were dressed like thugs and none of them were smiling as they all studied Max.

This didn't make any sense. Max couldn't understand why the four thugs would be here with the police if they were smuggling stolen artifacts; unless the police were in on the deal; or they were not real police. If that was the case then maybe the whole warehouse was in on the plan, but that was ridiculous because that would involve most of the town and that would not make sense. His head was spinning with thoughts that kept getting stranger and stranger. He couldn't believe that any stolen artifact would be worth enough for all of these people to get enough money for their part in the scheme. It had to be that Willie was involved in something by himself, and that he brought Max into it to have him take the fall while Willie escaped with the real artifacts. That was stranger than anything he had dreamed up yet. How could Willie have gotten to the crates over all the pallets of produce to remove whatever was hidden in them? Max kept thinking about the fact that Willie refused to sleep anywhere but in the bunk of his truck. Was he hiding something in there all this time and Max never even knew about it? Whatever it was it must have been pretty small because he didn't notice any large packages the night he sat in the bunk at the scale while Willie was inside the building. He began to have very bad feelings about Willie and thought that he just used him to get even for something that happened years before. What a jerk, he thought; what had he said that day; "If it's the last thing I do."

It seemed to be taking a long time to get the pry bar and while he waited the nervousness seemed to be affecting his bladder, and he started wondering if the group of people standing in front of him were experiencing the same problem, and if they would let him go to the bathroom; but just as he was about to ask, the guy sent to get the pry bar arrived and the "policeman "in charge took it and stepped up to the crate nearest him and began prying off the cover. As he began prying off the cover Max began having a second wave of paranoia. Maybe it took so long for the pry bar to arrive because the whole group was giving Willie time to get farther away. Maybe Willie was the leader of the whole operation and these guys just helped him escape. All these crazy thoughts flooded his brain as Max watched the man with the pry bar slowly open the crate.

Before he opened it completely he looked at Max and asked him again if he had any objections to them opening it.

"That's crazy!" Max shouted. "I told you they are not my crates, they belong to the guy that owns the truck. We have just waited ten minutes for someone to bring a pry bar and now you ask if I have any objections to having the crates opened."

"Just making sure you didn't change your mind about ownership and want us to get a search warrant. Possession is nine tenths of the law and you are the only person from this vehicle here, so technically that makes you responsible for the contents of the vehicle." As the policeman continued to pry the cover off the crate Max stated that he was a lawyer and was quite aware of what the law stated and did not state.

"Well, if you are a lawyer you might want to call yourself for representation." Then they all laughed at the guys attempt to be a comedian.

The crates were opened from the side away from Max and the covers were raised towards him so he couldn't see over them to the inside of the crates. As the first one was opened all of the group stepped forward and looked

inside and nodded; the same procedure was followed with
the second crate. After the second crate was opened and
they had all looked inside everyone except the "professor"
stepped back to form the semi-circle again. The professor
looked from the crate to Max and back to the crate, then
bending forward he reached into the crate while declaring
that he thought there was indeed something that belonged
to Max inside.

The "professor" removed a small package wrapped in
plain brown paper and tied with a string, and straightened
up to look at Max. Max was still unable to see what else,
if anything was in the crate because of the cover that was
blocking his view, but he did notice some straw on the
package he was being presented with, and assumed it was
packing material for whatever else was in the crate.

"That's not mine and I am not going to touch it!" Max
shouted as the guy handed him the package.

The professor looked at Max and said "This must be
yours; it has your name on it."

Max was frantic now and tried to remember if he had
ever given his name to anyone of these people since this
whole weird incident began. He couldn't remember that
he had, and when the professor turned the package over so
Max could see the other side he saw in bold black print his
full name. "Willie" was all he could think at the moment.

As he slowly reached for the package he wondered
how Willie could have possibly carried this much hatred
for him all these years, to go through all this trouble
to frame him for something like this, while he made
good his escape. He thought about his home in California
and his wife and wished desperately that he was there

with both of them at this very moment. He stared at the package as he took it from the hand that offered it to him. He wondered as he touched it what kind of artifact could be so soft, and as he untied the string and looked inside he was suddenly startled by a voice very close to his ear whispering, "Gotcha".

Max looked up from the stuffed toy skunk inside the paper wrapper to look into the face of his old friend smiling from ear to ear. "I told you I would get you back, even if it was the last thing I ever did."

Max felt someone take hold of his arm and looked to his left to see Sue standing there smiling, "I'm sorry, they made me promise not to say anything." Then she reached up and pulled his head down and kissed him. "Jean picked me up the day you left and the two of us have been kind of following you guys all the way back."

"But I've been talking to you at the house on the phone all the while we have been in the truck." He said.

"No, the phone has been transferred to my cell and you talked to me through that. It's complicated for you, but trust me I wasn't home when you talked to me." Sue held up her cell phone and said that it was not the time but that he really had to become more connected with the modern world.

"Well," Max said, "I guess that explains the mysterious click in the phone that I heard every time I called. I feel a little foolish thinking that some government group was tapping the phone and tracking my location."

Then he looked around at the faces in the group around him. As if on cue the serious looks disappeared and they all began laughing and talking at once. They all said the same thing, but used different words so the effect was an incoherent babble that roughly translated into the same thing; "It was Willies idea." After he slowly looked around the group from face to face Max had one thing on his mind and he reached down to take hold of the lid of one of the crates. He turned it so he could look inside then turned the other one so he could do the same. His imagination over what was in them had gone wild over the past couple days and now the red tinge of embarrassment returned to his face because all that was in them were oranges.

He looked at Willie and then at the bearded man who was laughing with the rest of them, then back at Willie. "What was all that talk about looted museums and stolen artifacts about?"

"Just that," Willie said. "I just used the power of suggestion to start you thinking that there was something sinister about those crates and let your imagination do the rest."

"OK, what was that letter that you slipped into your pocket that morning in the restaurant?"

Willie reached into his jeans pocket and pulled out the envelope; now quite crumpled and slightly torn and held it up for Max to see; "You mean this envelope? This is a letter for my insurance company signed by a doctor stating that I was healthy enough to drive. This is the doctor that signed it." He said and indicated the bearded man in the group facing them.

The look of confusion on Max's face caused another round of laughter from the group and Willie took hold of his arm and said, "I'll explain everything over dinner, but right now I want to introduce you to some people from town."

As Willie started talking Max had a sudden attack of anxiety that almost caused him to lose his balance. The skunk in the crate, the mysterious sudden appearance of Willie back in his life, a Minnesota doctor in California giving Willie a signed statement allowing him to drive a commercial vehicle, and finally Willie's long ago promise that he would get even if it was the last thing he did. It could only mean one thing and he stared at Willie hoping it wasn't true.

Max stood looking at Willie and noticed Jean peeking around his side smiling. He looked at the stuffed toy skunk in his hand and back at Willie and said in a very small voice filled with so much sincerity that it caught Willie off guard, "I'm sorry." Jean recovered first and said," Well it sure took you long enough to say it," then she reached up and forward with both arms and hugged him to her for a long friendship restoring hug. Max looked at Willie and said, "I truly am sorry."

"I wonder what our lives would have been like if you would have said that a long time ago," Willie said as he took Jeans place to give his friend a hug and a buddy punch in the shoulder.

"Well, I don't see a rewind button around here so we will probably never know the answer to that one, but I'll bet you probably have a few other questions; am I right?" The professor was talking as he closed the lid on the crate closest to him and the policeman did the same with the one closest to him.

"For the past thirteen years Willie has brought back two crates of oranges every week, and we have picked them up here every week; the difference this week is that it is his last delivery and he added a few things to make it memorable. He gives one case to me and the other case goes to the police department. I am head of the surgery department at the hospital where Willie was treated after his accident so many years ago. I specialize in childhood cancer and the oranges are for the children. The other case is given out to the officers on patrol and they hand them out to kids they see on their routes that look a little hungry, and maybe a little neglected. Both cases go to the kids and Willie refuses to take anything for them. He won't even let us acknowledge him publicly for the gifts. With co-operation from the growers, shippers and this company we are going to continue the program and expand it to other cities because that simple act of kindness from the officers and doctors has had such a great positive effect on the kids." He stopped talking and looked at Willie, who was blushing as red as a beet. "I don't know how much Willie has told you about his life but I sure felt honored that I happened to be in California on a conference visit when Willie needed to talk to me."

Willie gave him a grateful smile and then looked at Max, "Do you recognize any of these other hooligans?" He indicated the other "policemen", and thugs still standing in a half circle and now smiling and all looking a Max.

"I don't know? It's weird because they look familiar, but they are too young for me to possibly have met them before." Max looked from face to face and then at Willie.

Willie reached out and clasped the shoulder of one of the policemen near him. "This is Jeff you knew his father. Jeff's parents were married right after high school and then his dad got drafted. Jeff was born three weeks before his dad was killed in Vietnam. His dad also played football and put skunks in the back of pickup trucks."

As Max looked at the younger man that Willie had been talking about he realized why he looked familiar. He looked an awful lot like his dad; and Max looked at the other "thug" that he thought he knew and realized it was the son of one of the other guys who were in on the prank that had gone bad so many years ago.

Willie moved over to the other person Max had recognized and put his arm around his shoulder. This is Jim, His folks were married a few months after school and his dad also got drafted. Actually his dad and I went to basic training together. His dad died of cancer a couple years ago, and yes he used to play football and put skunks in pickup trucks too." These two aren't thugs or a police officer they are doctors in the hospital. I just asked them to dress up for this little drama I dreamed up.

The "policeman" that had been doing the talking as if he were in charge stepped forward and extended his hand to Max. "I'm a real cop; you evidently don't remember me but I also put skunks in the back of pickup trucks and played football. I guess I was the quiet one of the bunch."

Max looked at the man in front of him and there was a sudden burst of recognition. The "policeman was actually the third friend with Max that day. He was right, the guy was always around but never did say much. "Man, how times have changed us," and Max stepped forward and grabbed his outstretched hand and shook it with a double handed shake of friendship.

"We've all kind of been waiting for you to come back home but you just stayed in California being some old big shot lawyer." The "policeman stepped back and said that he and Willie probably had some catching up to do and that he and his men had to get back to work. He said he would probably see him around if he stayed a while; then the other men in uniform picked up a crate of oranges and left; but not before he gave Willie a look and a nod of his head; a look that Max thought was a little too sad for the moment.

The "professor" also said he had to get going and thanked Willie for the oranges, and said he would talk to him at his next appointment, then he followed the rest of the group out the door. "Funny," Max thought," they all made such a dramatic entrance coming from different directions and walking the length of the warehouse then they all leave by the same door right across the warehouse floor from where they were. They should all have been actors." Then he realized how bad he still had to go to the bathroom and told Willie that before there was any story time there was going to have to be bathroom time.

Willie laughed and pointed to a door down the warehouse and Max rushed towards it.

Jean, Sue and Willie talked until Max returned from the restroom, smiling a smile of relief and still carrying the stuffed toy skunk.

Willie laughed and said it looked like he had found a new friend. Max looked a little embarrassed but did not make any comment.

The warehouse was very quiet after all the noise and confusion of the day when there had been trucks being unloaded and loaded, people coming and going in different directions and forklifts racing around moving product. For a brief moment none of them spoke and there was no other sound in the building, Willie looked around the building and Max could see the sadness in his eyes.

"Is this really your last load, or was that just another part of this little play you put on for me?" Max looked at Willie, and then at Jean and Sue sensing there was more to the situation than he had been told.

Willie looked at him and smiled. "Yes, this is the last load; I'm going from here directly to the RV dealer and trading for my new ride, to start my new life. It will probably take a while to get the deal done so why don't you and Sue take the jeep and do some touring, and then we will meet you at the house. It's been a while since you've been there but I think you can still find your way."

When Sue and Max had left to get Max's things out of the truck and tour the town Jean and Willie stood in silence for a while, as Willie looked around the warehouse. It was a strange feeling thinking that he would not be coming back here with a load next week. He slowly moved to the dock and picked up his load locks and began to carry them to the front of the trailer as he always did to secure the stacks of pallets. He had only taken a couple steps when he realized there were no pallets this time. He turned and laid the locks on the floor against the wall and exited the trailer, and pulled the chain to secure the dock plate in the down position.

"I suppose I could try to sell those locks for a couple bucks, but I'll just leave them in the trailer and whoever buys it will think they are getting a deal." Willie looked at Jean and reached out to draw her close for a homecoming hug that he got every week when he returned from his trip. As he held her he said, "Well, I think I pulled this little caper off rather nicely. Now let's get out of here and get rid of the "other woman" so I can spend my time with the real woman in my life." Jean looked up into his eyes and hugged him a little closer, and they both had tears in their eyes as Jean turned to exit through the employee entrance towards the car parking lot, and Willie went out the exit to get into his truck for the last time.

As Jean opened the door a warm summer breeze blew across her face. She stepped to the side and let the door close behind her. The sun was warm and the parking lot was nearly deserted, she leaned against the building and let the sun warm her after being in the refrigerated warehouse. She looked around the parking lot and noticed that the office end still had several vehicles parked in it but this end was empty except for two cars and an ugly yellow-green or green-yellow pickup shining in the afternoon sun. The warehouse workers having started early in the morning left quickly after the last truck had been unloaded and the product was tagged and put away. In a short while the crew that picks the products and sorts them into the loads to be shipped would arrive, and the quiet warehouse would again be the scene of another forklift ballet. The two cars belonged to the clean-up crew and they would be leaving soon.

As she leaned against the building and looked at that pickup truck shining in the sunlight she thought about the fact that for almost a half century there had been two things that had been stable in her life; that ugly truck and the man that owned it.

She thought about her friends who had left in their jeep to explore the old hometown and fill in the time until Willie finished the deal trading his semi for an RV. She was excited about an evening with them which had been too long in coming.

She thought about the day so long ago when Willie had left her at the school then returned with a new dress and asked her to still be his date.

She thought about the time after the prom when Willie and Max had avoided each other completely the rest of the school year. After graduation Sue and Max had moved to California and Willie had been drafted into the army and she had been left alone for a couple years with only letters from Willie to support her.

The dress Willie had bought was still in the closet at home. She had never been able to get rid of it through all the years since that faraway time. The one she had originally picked out and spent all her money on, having it altered and fitted so it looked just right, had never been picked up from Sue's house. She had gone there from the school and changed and waited for Willie; and she told Sue to get rid of it because she didn't want to see it again.

The dress Willie had bought was the one that stays in every dress shop after all the other dresses are sold. It seems that the shops buy one very plain and unattractive gown just to make the other dresses look better. That was the dress Willie had bought. He walked into the store and said he needed a dress for his date to wear to the prom, and told the salesperson about what size he needed and they brought it out and he said put it in a box, I'll take it.

The dress had been an awful design and the color had been close to the color of his truck being an off green, and it had a large gaudy bow on the left shoulder; but Jean hadn't cared. She put it on and pinned it in a few places to make it fit better and that night, at the dance she felt like the luckiest girl in the world; she knew she was the happiest; she was at a fancy ball with her prince charming. "Willie, what would I ever do without you?"

Jean pushed away from the wall and walked to the ugly pickup, and as she walked around the front to get to the drivers side she dragged her hand across the hood feeling its familiar shape and curves. She continued tracing the side of the truck as she walked to the door, got in, and began driving towards the exit gate of the factory lot. As she went through the gate she reached into the case that held the cassette tapes and randomly picked one out. She took it out of the case and inserted it into the player. The music played and the singer sang about seeing paradise by the dashboard light and she smiled; remembering.

While Jean was leaving out one door Willie was going out the other side of the building and he too let the door shut behind him and leaned against the building wall. Although the sun was shining on the other side of the building, and his side was in the shade, it was still warm on the side Willie was on. He took a moment to look around. The familiar sight of the parking lot looked a little different from the perspective of being the last time he would exit the building to get in his truck and go home for the weekend.

He could see through the passenger side mirror that Max and Sue were still there getting his things out of the truck so he leaned against the building, as Jean had done on the other side, and just took in the scene before him.

This side of the building was in the shadow of the afternoon and despite the warm summer day he felt a chill. He stuck his hands deep into his blue jean pockets and leaned against the wall behind him. He thought back over the years and wished he would have called Max a long time ago, but he hadn't and so he thought tomorrow they would go fishing and make up for lost time by making some new memories.

When he heard the passenger door close on the semi he started to walk to the cab, and as he walked he automatically checked the condition of the tires and the trailer as he always did when he walked to the cab to drive away from a dock. He got in the cab, started the truck and pulled a short distance away from the dock; then stopped. He got out of the cab and walked to the back of the trailer and swung the two doors closed; as he flipped the last latch into place he thought to himself, well, that's it, now it's somebody else's worry.

Once again he walked the distance from the back of the trailer to the cab of the truck and climbed in. He released the brakes, put the truck in gear, and started driving towards the gate for the last time. As he drove across the parking lot he reached into the box of cassettes and picked one, removed it from the case and inserted it into the player. The singer started singing about how they love to watch her strut and he looked at Jeans picture on the dash and said quietly, "Yes I do."

As he approached the gate the security guard lowered the gate forcing him to stop. The guard then came out of his guardhouse and stood beside the truck until Willie opened the door. Willie couldn't understand why the guard forced him to stop; they never stopped him on his other deliveries when he passed through the gate. He was not especially close friends with any of the guards. He had exchanged greetings with them on occasion and was a bit surprised when he reached up his hand and with real heartfelt emotion said, "Good luck my friend; it's been a pleasure and an honor to know you."

Willie didn't know what to think of this and got out of the truck to be on the same level with the guard. He grasped his outstretched hand and shook it. "Thanks, "he said "that was nice of you to say that, good luck to you."

Willie climbed back into the cab and waving to the guard he once again released the brakes, put the transmission in gear and started through the gate. He was so used to turning left when he exited the lot to go home he already had his turn signal on and was starting to turn the wheel when he corrected himself, put the right signal on, and turned towards the RV dealership where Jean was waiting for him to clean his things out of the truck and pick up their new "rig".

Sue and Max left the lot turning left; the direction of Willies house but also the direction to the farm Max had grown up on. When they reached the place Max had called home he almost drove past without noticing it. The place was totally changed and he couldn't see any of the old familiar landmarks he remembered; or thought he remembered. He slowed the Jeep and tried to remember the buildings and trees and all the other things that he had pictured in his mind on the occasions when he thought back to the days of trout fishing and long walks home. Nothing was left of the place he grew up in. The out buildings had all been removed along with the old farm house; in their place was a modern rambler with an attached three car garage. Funny, he thought, three car garage for a couple with no children. The trees had also been removed or had fallen down; he thought about the big oak and maple trees that used to grace the yard that had been replaced with pines and bushes, and wished he could have them back.

They continued to drive out into the country and nothing was familiar. Where he used to know where to turn just by the buildings, or an old tree, he now had to watch the road signs. Even that wasn't a sure guide because the county had been zoned and now instead of county road signs there were streets and avenues that didn't make sense to him at all. Fifteen years since there last visit home had sure made a difference. Eventually he adjusted to the changes and just let his old feelings steer the vehicle. He made a turn onto a side road and found they were heading down the road that led to the old swimming hole. When they arrived at the spot that had been the scene of so many good times they found that that too had changed. A flood had changed the creek so there was no longer a large deep hole there, but only a wide spot in the stream. One thing still remained of the days when they had partied at this spot. An old bent and dying oak tree, that had been old and dying when they were young.

"I can't believe that tree is still there; at least one thing is here from our past." Then he looked at Sue and said, "Make that two things, I still love you like I did back then." He leaned over put his arm around her shoulders and kissed her. Then they sat lost in their own thoughts and enjoyed the late afternoon sunshine, with Sue resting her head on his shoulder and the both of them seventeen again.

After a long stretch with neither of them saying anything Sue broke the silence and said, "Let's get out and touch the old tree just to prove that it's real."

Max looked at her then at the tree and back at her; "what do you mean? Of course it's real."

"I know, but let's just get out and stand by it," she said

"OK," Max said but don't expect me to climb it like I used to, because there is no swimming hole to jump into anymore."

They got out of the Jeep and walked the short distance to the tree, holding hands and remembering. Sue pointed across the creek at the large cliff face on the other side, where kids used to, and it looked like still did, carve their initials into the sandstone to proclaim their undying love for each other. "There's something else from the past that hasn't disappeared." Sue was pointing high up on the rock wall, almost to the very top, where two hearts had been carved side by side. One said Sue and Max and the other said Jean and Willie. "They are still the highest ones there." She said. "You two were pretty cocky after you put those up there. You were right though; nobody will top them." They stood holding hands and leaned against each other remembering until the sound of an approaching vehicle brought them back to the present.

The vehicle pulled off the road and parked a short distance from the Jeep. It was full of young kids and it appeared they were there to party. The old spot still held the same magic for the young even without the swimming hole; maybe it was the old oak tree that drew the young kids and not the creek. The kids seemed upset that there were two "old" people sitting by their tree and interrupting their party. "Yes, Max said some things never change. Remember how upset the kids would get if there were some "older" people here fishing when they wanted to party?"

"Yes, and we would sit quietly in the vehicle and wait them out; and were not as rude as these kids are." The kids had gotten out of their vehicle and were standing around it making remarks loud enough for Max and Sue to hear about how older people didn't belong there. "Let's just sit here awhile longer and make them wait their turn." Sue was on the defensive and Max liked her attitude.

"Yea," Max said, "after all, everybody knows how slow 'old people' are."

After a while they got up, brushed their pants off and walked to the Jeep. They didn't say anything to the kids who turned their backs to them as they walked past. But before they reached the Jeep Sue couldn't contain herself; she turned towards the nearest person and said, "See that heart way up there on the top right? Well, I'm Sue and this is Max, that heart is older than a lot of your parents and you should have a little more respect for your elders."

The people from the other vehicle didn't know what to say and they just stood looking at the "old" couple as they got into their Jeep and drove away down the road.

After they had driven down the road a ways they looked at each other and began laughing. They laughed so hard that Tears came to their eyes and Max had to pull over.

"Where did that come from, back there?" Max asked after they had regained their composure.

"I don't know; it just had to be done." And they laughed again. Sitting in Willies Jeep on the side of the road they laughed, and when they stopped laughing they each took a deep breath and leaned back into the seats.

"That felt good." Then they laughed again because they had both said the exact same thing at the exact same time. "We better stop this or someone will see us and think we are stoned," Sue said.

"Yea, we better get back to town," Max said and started driving. They had driven quit a few miles before the occasional giggle stopped and by them they were back in town. They drove down the street Sue grew up on and past her childhood home. Sue commented that the place really hadn't changed except that the new owners had resided it and that she didn't like the color.

They drove by the high school and Max slowed down. Sue asked what was the problem and Max said, "Shouldn't there be a message on the marquee about the reunion?" Then he looked at Sue and said, "There isn't a reunion, is there?"

"Actually, no," she said, "the story about me throwing the invitation in the trash was Jeans idea."

Max shook his head and said, "Boy, he had everybody involved in this little scheme of his; didn't he?"

"Well," Sue said "he did put some thought into it, but then he had time to think. Being alone in that truck was probably not a good thing for someone with a mind like Willie. Let's drive up to the scenic overlook and we can watch Willie and Sue make the deal on their new RV; I'll tell you the story Jean told me, about Willie, on the trip back here."

They drove up the curvy winding road leading out of town and parked in the overlook, from where they could look down on the town. They could see the dealership and could make out the form of Willies semi and trailer. They could see the tiny figures of the people moving around, and now that it was getting dark and the lights were coming on, they could see the shine of the chrome on the new RV parked next to it. They could also make out an ugly green-yellow or yellow-green pickup parked in the lot. "You know, even from this distance that thing is ugly; but shiny," Max said, then he chuckled to himself.

He was still chuckling when he looked over at Sue and noticed that she was crying. He stopped his laughter and turned back to the windshield and the scene far below. "So, tell me," he said

Sue took a deep breath and wiped her eyes with a Kleenex, leaned her head back and took another deep breath. "Remember when you first saw Willie in the truck parking lot? That night when you called you made a comment about how dirty and dusty his truck was and that it wasn't like the old Willie you used to know? Well, his truck had been sitting in that parking lot for a month because he had been in the hospital.

Jean didn't just drive to California to pick me up; she had been there for weeks. Willie got sick on his trip out and managed to get his load delivered, but ended up in the hospital, where they discovered he has cancer. When he found out he wouldn't be able to drive for awhile, if ever, he called Jean and told her he wanted her to drive his pickup out to him. The cancer had affected his heart and that was what had made him sick and put him in the hospital. He wanted to see you again, but didn't want you to see him in the hospital, so he waited until he found out if he would be able to drive and then came up with this goofy idea to get you to go with him in the truck, and me to ride back with Jean.

When he found out his doctor friend from the children's hospital was in California for a conference he contacted him and together they came up with this plan to get both Willie and his truck back to Minnesota.

The doctor, Jean and I were at the weigh station that night you two stopped. Willie needed daily treatments and the doctor set up his equipment there. Willie used that weigh station parking lot to sleep in on his trips because it was quiet and he was never bothered by a lot of other trucks. The sign went from open to closed so no other trucks would interrupt them. Willie and the scale master were good friends and when he heard about Willies trouble he was more than willing to help him out"

"Well, that explains the flash of green I saw behind the shed," said Max

"We were also at the truck stop you stopped at last night. Jean said you saw her and Willie talking but didn't think you recognized her.

Jean said Willie talked about contacting you quiet a lot over the years, but things never worked out. He was always waiting for you to call and apologize, but you never did." Sue stopped talking and looked back at the scene far below.

As Max watched the activity in the parking lot he realized that the stupidest thing he had ever done was not getting involved with that stupid prank, but was letting the prank destroy their friendship by not talking to Willie and apologizing. Their whole lives had slipped away and now it might be too late to make amends.

"I guess that explains a lot of the things I wandered about on the trip. I wandered how someone as active as Willie had been could become so slow in his movements and stiff in their walk, but age and sickness does that to a person. I was really stupid for not guessing what was going on. I didn't think from the way he talked about his truck that he would give it up voluntarily." Max felt a strong desire to be fishing beside his old friend again and made a promise to himself that he would try to make up as much of the lost time as he could.

"Actually, they have owned the RV for three years," Sue said, "what they are trading the semi for is the renovation work that the dealership has put into it. Willie had the hospital and the dealership work together to make it into a mobile cancer treatment center for children with cancer. They are going to take it to see a couple places they have wanted to visit to make sure it works the way it is supposed to and then they are going to donate it to the hospital, so that kids with cancer will be able to take trips and still get their treatments. Willie says he won't need it because he is going to beat his cancer just like he has beaten every other problem in his life."

While they were watching the scene below one of the figures suddenly collapsed to the ground and the others stopped what they were doing and rushed to the spot.

Without saying anything Max immediately started the Jeep and began driving down the curvy road; although neither of them voiced their thoughts both Sue and Max imagined it was Willie who had fallen. While they were heading for the scene below they saw flashing lights approaching from the direction of the hospital, and other emergency vehicles coming from several directions.

When they arrived at the RV dealership the ambulance had already left and the several police vehicles had turned off their lights and sirens. There were a few people standing in a group near Willies pickup and Max turned the Jeep in that direction. When they got closer they recognized Jean standing by the driver's door talking to one of the policemen who had been in the warehouse just a few hours before. She looked as if the life had been drained out of her and she was unable to function or move on her own.

Even before the Jeep had came to a complete stop Sue had her door open and was stepping out, in a hurry to get to her friend in her time of distress. She had wished Jean would have called her when Willie had his first trouble in California and now that she was here, and able to be with Jean when she needed support, she couldn't get to her fast enough.

The policeman that had been supporting Jean, and trying to get her to give up the idea that she could drive herself to the hospital, stepped aside when he saw Sue approaching. When Jean recognized her friend she seemed to regain some of her composure and reached out to Sue for support. Sue put one arm around her waist and with the other hand supporting Jean's elbow she led her around to the passenger side of the pickup. Max opened the door and Sue helped Jean into the seat, and then ran around to the driver's door and got in. The keys were in the ignition and without saying a word to anyone she started the vehicle and drove away in the direction of the hospital.

Max stood in the parking lot and looked around at the faces of the people there. The officer that had been talking to Jean was the same one that had done most of the talking in the warehouse. He had tears trickling down his cheeks and in a voice that quivered with emotion he said "His heart stopped." Then he turned and walked to his squad car and with lights and siren blaring he sped off towards the hospital.

The other officers then approached Max and began filling him in on what they knew of his condition. Max listened as they told him that Willie had groaned and fell down and that one of the employees of the dealership was on the emergency medical team. They had used CPR to keep his heart going until the ambulance arrived and he was still not conscious when they left. Max thanked them and got in the Jeep and hurried to the hospital.

When Max entered the emergency waiting area of the hospital he spotted Sue talking to the officer from the dealership and rushed to her side. They didn't say anything they just hugged each other tightly.

Willie had said that getting back at Max for the skunk, with a prank to match, was one thing he was going to do. Even if it was the last thing he ever did.

"Willie, you old fool; you didn't have to take yourself so literally," Max thought as he stood hugging Sue.

Max watched a kaleidoscope of pictures pass from his memory, past his mind's eye, and fade back into memory. Two small boys playing too late into the evening so one of them had to walk home in the dark. The sights he remembered when it was him walking alone with only his dog for company. The night he heard a bobcat scream in the distance causing him to run the rest of the way to his house. The memory of watching Willie disappear into the darkness when they had played too long at Max's house. The innocent knowledge that he would see him the next day. Now, as he stood holding his wife he wished with his whole being that he could have that childhood certainty back.

Sue stood with her arms wrapped tightly around her husband. Her eyes were closed and her mind was in a turmoil. She listened to the strong beating of Max's heart and felt a terrible pain for her friend Jean. She wished with every part of her that Jean would be able to hear that sound echoing in Willie's chest when they hugged again.

After standing in each other's arms for a long time they eventually let each other go and took a deep breath. They looked around and spotted a couple chairs in a corner out of the busy part of the room and they walked to them and sat down. They sat in silence for several minutes not knowing what to do or what to say. Max felt as lost as he had that day so many years ago, when he was in this very hospital wondering if he would see his friend and be able to make up for lost time with him.

After a long wait Jean came through a set of double doors that led to the treatment area of the hospital. She slowly walked towards them when she saw them sitting there. She looked ashen and tired, but managed a smile as she sank into a chair facing them. "Well, they got his heart going and he is awake. It is going to be a long night and the hospital gave me a bed in his room so why don't you two go to the house and get some rest. We will have to postpone that homecoming dinner for a few days, but make yourselves at home and tomorrow we will know more."

They all got up and without saying anything they hugged and held each other for a long time. When the hug finally ended Sue wiped her eyes and said in a small voice," OK, we'll talk to you in the morning." Then Jean turned and walked back through the doors she had entered through and they turned to the exit door of the hospital leading to the parking lot.

They walked in silence to the Jeep and both got in without saying anything. They were both lost in their own memories and as Max drove to Willies house he again thought of the time of innocence and fun when he and Willie were growing up. He didn't give any thought to the road signs or which way to turn he just did it out of instinct. When he got to the driveway at Willies house he slowed for the turn and looked down the road in the direction of his boyhood home. He saw in the distance the all-night yard light marking the house he grew up in. He again thought of the many nights he had walked that road in the dark before anyone had all-night lights. The only lights were the fireflies in the fields and, if he was lucky the moon and some stars.

As he turned into the driveway the lights swung in an arch lighting up the garden and the garden shed. The garden was just as big as it had been the day he buried the fishing worms after Willies accident. The garden shed was still in the same spot and still well painted. He could imagine the fork was still hanging on the wall in the same spot it always hung. He thought about the day he buried the worms, there had been times after that when he had been with Willie while he buried worms, and many, many times before, but the day of Willies accident was the time he thought about now.

"The doctors warned him that they didn't think he was strong enough to make the trip home driving his truck." The sound of Sue's voice brought him back to reality and Max turned to look at her. "He was so determined to go through with his stupid plan to get you back here that the doctors finally agreed that the stress of not letting him do it would be worse than the stress of driving, so they let him do it. They only agreed to it if he promised to have his treatments and get checked out every day. Jean, the doctor and I checked him every night and he was doing so good. I can't understand why this happened now." Then she broke down and started crying; something she had managed to fight off until she saw the house her and Jean had laughed in earlier that day.

After parking the Jeep and sitting in silence for a couple minutes Max reached over and took Sue's hand and squeezed it." Let's go in and we can sit and talk and maybe get some sleep." Sue looked at him and nodded.

When they entered the house Max stopped and looked around. The remodeling had changed the interior some but he still recognized it as the place he had been in so many times in the past. One thing he noticed right away was a large banner draped across the opposite wall. He read the words and looked at the picture, and smiled down at Sue. They both slipped off their shoes and walked to the sofa and sat down. The remote for the TV was on the coffee table in front of them but neither of them reached for it. They just sunk down into the softness of the sofa and sat in silence.

After a few minutes had passed Max turned his head and looked at Sue. Reaching for her hand he said, "I love you." Then he said "You've often said that it would be nice to retire someplace other than California. I know that you would like to move back here so what would you say if I said we should do it now, instead of waiting a couple more years like we had planned? This whole incident has shown me how unpredictable life is and that there is no guarantee we have a couple years."

Sue looked at him through eyes red from crying and asked, "What about our jobs?"

"What about them?" Max said. "We have worked long enough; we have enough to live comfortably so why not enjoy it while we can? Graveyards are full of people who worked themselves to death thinking they would quit in "a couple years". Let's go to bed and sleep on it, and tomorrow we'll drive in to the hospital and while we are in town we can look around to see what is available to buy."

Sue nodded her head and they went into the room Jean had told Sue was to be theirs while they were staying there.

After a restless night Max and Sue got up and prepared to drive into town to the hospital. Neither of them talked much and both of them were in a hurry to find out how Willie was doing. When they arrived at the hospital they went to the front desk and inquired about Willie. The lady working behind the desk smiled and said, "You know, I was quite a lot younger the last time you asked about that guy." Max didn't understand what she was talking about but she explained that she had just started working at the hospital with Jean as a candy striper when the wall had fallen at the construction site and Willie had been brought to the hospital. "Jean and I had both been attracted to that handsome young boy; but Jean was the one that landed him." She pointed behind them and said," There's Jean now; you can ask her yourselves how he's doing."

They turned and walked to meet Jean in the middle of the waiting room. Sue reached out and hugged her and Max put his arm around her shoulder and pulled her close with a hug. "So, how's he doing?" they both asked at once.

Jean looked better than she had the night before, but she still looked very tired and confused. "I am so glad you two are here." She said. "I wanted to call you when we were in California but Willie wouldn't let me. The stubborn old coot didn't want to spoil his plan. He's doing very well, and the doctors say he shouldn't be in here very long. You know how he was when he was young and he has not changed any. He wanted to leave today but there is no way he's up to that. This time I'm not letting him get out of here until the doctors are sure he's up to it. He conned me in California but he isn't going to con me here." She stopped talking and seemed to drift off into her thoughts, so Max and Sue let her have her time for reflection. When she looked at Sue and smiled Sue asked if he was awake and if they could see him. Jean said he was sleeping and would probably sleep for awhile because the doctors had given him medication to relax him.

Max said she needed to get away from the hospital for a while, and they agreed that breakfast would make her feel better. So they left the hospital and got in the Jeep and drove to a local restaurant.

When they entered the restaurant Max looked around but didn't recognize any of the other customers. The business had been there when he was young but it had changed hands and been remodeled so he didn't feel familiar with any of it. Jean led the way to a booth and they all ordered coffee when the waitress arrived. They said they would order breakfast in a little while, but for now all they wanted was coffee.

They sat in the booth and talked and eventually the subject of moving back came up. Jean's face lit up and she grabbed Sue's hand and said "Really?"

Max said he had brought the subject up last night but that they hadn't talked it through yet. Jean was so excited it was almost like she had decided for them. She said she had thought about them coming back for a long time but had eventually given up on the idea after so many years had passed.

Max said that they really would like to leave the stress of California and that they could sell their house out there for quite a lot of money. They ordered breakfast and ate and talked and while they were finishing their coffee a man from a table near them got up and approached their booth.

"Excuse me for interrupting your conversation, but I overheard what you said about moving back here. I didn't recognize you at first but now I know you're Max and you're Sue. You probably don't remember me but I was in the class behind Max in school. Anyway, I thought that I would tell you that I just talked to the couple that bought your old place, and that they have decided to do what you are thinking of doing and moving back to the east coast where they grew up. They said they were going to list the farm with a realtor today. Maybe if you hurry you can talk to them before they do. It might save you the realtor fee."

Max stood up and shook the man's hand and thanked him for the information. When he sat back down and looked from Sue to Jean he was smiling broadly and said, "Well, I guess that was a pretty strong indication that we are moving back. Maybe this news will help Willie get out of the hospital faster. You know, I have a feeling that things are going to turn out alright."